Mistress Jennet

MARJORIE HULL

First published 1997 by
WINCKLEY PRESS
5 Winckley Street
Preston PR1 2AA

ISBN 0-907769-23-3

Set in 12 on 13 Goudy
Designed and typeset by Winckley Press
Printed and bound in Great Britain

About the Author

Although she was not born in Preston, Marjorie Hull has lived in the town for over forty years and considers herself to be as much a Prestonian as anyone else. She is a great lover of history and it was when doing some research on Preston's past that she realised what a great potential was there for writing a book. 'Mistress Jennet' is the result – with more titles to follow.

Marjorie Hull is a mature lady who loves animals and nature, as well as pottering about in her small garden. She engages in a number of other activities such as painting, flower arranging, crocheting and many other passions too numerous to mention.

Dedication

To my daughter,
Marjorie Haw,
for unfailing help
and encouragement

Acknowledgements

To Jane Kneen and the Sealed Knot Society

PRESTON 1648

CHAPTER ONE

The blustery wind howled mournfully around the farm buildings, stirring the thatched roofs with eerie whisperings and whistling down the farmhouse chimneys.

It was a late February day in the year 1642. The farm was close by the village of Broughton near Preston in Lancashire. It had been a long hard winter and judging by the continuing bad weather, it wasn't over yet.

John Gregson, tenant farmer, rose that morning more reluctantly than was his wont, feeling as tired as when he had retired to bed the evening before.

He emerged from his bed-chamber next to the kitchen, rubbing his hands to restore the circulation. He found the servant-girl, Mary, on her knees before the fire-place, blowing the piled up wood with a pair of bellows.

The kitchen was cold and this did not improve Master Gregson's already uncertain temper.

He glanced around the kitchen and seeing no sign of his daughter, Jennet, asked the girl, "Where is your mistress? Why has she not seen to the fire before this, and where is my breakfast?"

Mary, startled, dropped the bellows and scrambled to her feet. "Ee, Maister, she has not yet risen. I wor just trying to get things started." She stirred the fire and began to fry the morning bacon, but her master bade her go and waken her mistress. "T'is not like her to lie abed." he growled.

Laying aside the pan upon the hob, Mary hurried up the narrow stairs to Jennet's small chamber under the eaves.

"Mistress Jennet!" she gasped. "Thi mun rise at once. The maister be calling for thi' and he be fair cross thi's not up betimes to get his breakfast." Seeing Jennet open her eyes and stir beneath the bed-covers, she hastened down to finish frying the bacon.

"She be awake, Maister," she reported, "and will be down presently." He grunted in obvious disapproval of his daughter's tardiness and sat down at the table.

The kitchen, which was living room as well, was a fairly large one, with dark, sooty beams from which were hanging various hams and haunches of bacon together with bunches of herbs which Jennet had grown in her small garden. The fireplace at which Mary was standing, was large too, with a huge iron pot hanging from a hook which could be drawn to one side of the fire, and a hob at the other.

Mary set the frying pan upon this latter and bringing a large jug from the shelves at the opposite side of the room upon which were set out cooking and eating utensils, began to pour out the morning ale into the horn cups on the table.

Old Jess and Simple Jack came in just then, their faces red and shining from their morning sluice at the pump in the yard. They stood waiting while Mary set out the slices of bacon and hunks of bread, and after a short blessing from the master, they sat down and fell to with a will.

Up in her room Jennet rose quickly, her mind still full of the dream she had just been having as Mary had awakened her. She seemed to be in a beautiful, warm room with a bright fire crackling in the grate and there was a table spread with a sumptuous feast in silver dishes on a snowy cloth. Rich hangings covered the walls and sitting at the head of the table a nebulous figure, a man she thought, who rose to greet her as she came towards him. She could not make out his features nor tell if it was anyone she knew. She thought that he was richly dressed but here she had woken up and the dream had faded.

Roused from her musings by the cold in the bare little room, she hurriedly poured out water from the ewer into the earthen dish which stood on a small chest, the only furniture in the room apart from her small straw-filled pallet. Quickly she washed and dried her face and hands and pulled her old brown woollen dress over her undershift, smoothing it's worn folds and gazed ruefully at the frayed ends at cuffs and hem and the many darned and patched places. She had only one other dress, rich dark blue when it was new, but sadly faded now with many washings. She wore it for church on Sundays or going to market.

It would be nice if Father would let her buy a length of cloth to make another dress, she'd worn this one almost every day for three years, since she was fourteen, and she'd naturally grown a lot since then. It was getting too small, the threadbare fabric stretching over her rapidly developing figure. Soon, even Father would have to admit, it would become almost immodest. She would like another colour, too, perhaps green to go with her eyes, although they were not exactly green, more hazel with flecks of green and gold.

Sighing, she took up her comb and hastily dragged it through her long brown hair, smoothing it down with her hands before setting her white cap on it.

When she got downstairs, her father and the two farmhands were rising from the table. John turned and glared at his daughter.

"You'll have to do better than this, my lass," he said sternly, "tis daylight already and the cows should have been milked an hour since."

"I am sorry, Father," Jennet answered meekly, "I slept ill last night, - I do not know why I was so restless."

"I trust you are not sickening?"

"Nay Father, I am well and I will soon be forward with my chores."

"Well, be off and see to the milking then and do not be tardy again. Jack will help you and then he can take the cows into the pasture. We will be ploughing the long meadow while 'tis still fine and Jack may clean out the shippon." He went out without further words, followed by old Jess, who muttered a gruff "Good morning," as he went.

Simple Jack stood twisting his battered hat as he waited for Jennet to swallow a hasty bite and a drink. Leaving Mary to clear away and wash the bowls and cups, with instructions as to what she must do after, Jennet took down her shawl from the peg behind the door and wrapped it warmly around her head and shoulders. With Jack at her heels, she stepped out and struggled across the yard to the shippon, the wind threatening to tear the shawl from her.

In the comparative warmth of the shippon the five cows moved restlessly. They turned their heads towards Jennet and Jack as they came in, looking reproachfully at the two. They lowed plaintively, their swollen udders causing discomfort.

Jennet settled herself on the stool, leaning her forehead against Dewdrop's warm, gently heaving flank, and soon the milk was sloshing rhythmically into the pail. Jack did the same at the other end of the line of cows. The sound of the milk squirting and the regular breathing of the cow almost lulled Jennet to sleep. She still felt tired after her restless, dream racked night, and again the memory of the last dream came to her. It was all so strange. What was the matter with her lately? She seemed to be having a lot of these strange dreams and nearly always about the same sort of thing. What had she to do with scenes like that? It seemed as far from her own simple, hard working existence, as the nearby town of Preston was from King Charles's 'sinful court', as her father phrased it.

And who was the man she had seen in the dream? She was sure she had never met such a person in her life. Nor was ever likely to, she thought ruefully. Such people were not numbered among their limited circle of acquaintances,

She was roused from her musings by the swishing of Dewdrop's tail and the clanking of pails. She realised guiltily that she had stopped the milking and the cow's head was turned round towards her. The animal was regarding her with puzzled and reproachful brown eyes. Turning round, she saw that Jack had finished milking two of the cows and was moving on to a third. Quickly, she finished Dewdrop and moved on to the remaining cow. When all were finished Jack led the animals out to the small pasture near the house. Then he helped her to carry the pails of milk into the dairy adjoining the kitchen where they emptied them into the waiting churns.

"Thank you, Jack," she said, smiling gratefully at the lad. "You have been very helpful. Now you must get on with cleaning out the shippon as my Father instructed." He flushed with pleasure at her praise and hastened off to start his chores.

Jennet fed the pigs and chickens, turning them into the small enclosure beside the shippon.

In the house, Mary was hard at work sweeping, scrubbing and dusting. She was just starting on Master Gregson's room as Jennet came in, so her mistress began her twice-weekly baking on the newly scrubbed table. She made pies and set them in the oven beside the wood fire. The bread dough, covered with a clean cloth, was put in the hearth to rise.

As she worked, Jennet wondered how she could pluck up enough courage to ask her father about the cloth for a new dress. She knew he had something on his mind for he seemed preoccupied lately. She thought he was working too hard for he seemed always tired, although he would never admit it. Never an easy man to live with, he was rigid in his views, and had his own firmly fixed ideas on everything, especially his religion. Since her mother died in childbirth when Jennet was seven he seemed to withdraw even further into himself, and had brought up his daughter quietly and without fuss, as many another man could not have done. There had been other children, but all of them had died as babies, including the boy whose birth had caused her mother's death and who had quietly slipped from life a few days later. She knew her father loved her but, she thought ruefully, he was generally chary of showing his affection. She wished he would sometimes.

Her childhood had been lonely, but there was the life at the farm and looking after the menfolk and the animals to keep her occupied. When she was ten he sent her twice a week to have lessons with the curate at Broughton Church. She learnt to read and write and some arithmetic and then the lessons ceased for Master Gregson reckoned that was enough for a girl to know. there were not many girls, or boys for that matter, who could boast that much education, Not unless they were rich and noble.

Jennet wished there was more reading matter to practise on for Master Gregson would have only the Bible and John Calvin "Institutes" in the house.

Of course, there was the weekly news-letter brought by the carrier every week - she looked forward to that - but lately, the news in it was not good and not very interesting to a young girl, with reports of this or that gentleman mustering men and arms either for the Parliament or the King. Sometimes, her father would not let her even read it, but would retire to his room with it, coming out some time later in a foul mood, irritably refusing to answer her queries as to its contents, except to mutter that it was not a woman's business to know about these things.

She felt these rebuffs keenly, feeling that at seventeen he would have thought her grown up enough and indeed, intelligent enough to discuss things with. She should have know better- to a man such as he, she was just a child and female at that, to be ordered about and corrected, cared for and protected too, but never, never, to be treated as an equal. So ran her rebellious thoughts until with a shake of her head she resolved to banish them and think of something more pleasant. Tomorrow was Market Day at Preston and she would be taking the cheese and butter she had made, with eggs from the chickens and churns of milk and buttermilk to sell in the market square.

This was the highlight of the week for Jennet, giving her perhaps her only contact with people other than those at Gregson's Farm, and the visits of the carrier with the weekly news-letter.

Many times during the past winter she had been unable to go, for the lanes leading to the town had been blocked with snowdrifts, or so mired up with heavy rains they could not get through. But now Spring was on its way, surely they could look forward to better weather. Her father usually insisted that if he could not take her himself, one of the men should go with her. It was dangerous in these troublous times, he said, for a young maid to go abroad alone, so although he could ill spare his hands, either Jess or Jack should accompany her. She wondered which one it would be on the morrow.

Mary came in at this point and bobbed a curtsey, saying that she had finished all that Mistress Jennet had asked her to do and could she go now as Broughton Church had just struck the hour of noon? Jennet gave her assent and waved to the thirteen-year-old as she ran off through the home pasture.

She looked after the girl affectionately. She was a good girl and a reliable worker and had been working for them for over a year now. She came in every morning from Broughton Village to help with the household tasks and sometimes gave a hand in the dairy.

Putting some bread and cheese and buttermilk into a basket, Jennet took it to her father and Jess in the long meadow, giving Jack his on the way, where he was cleaning out the shippon. Thankfully, she noticed that the harsh wind had died down somewhat and the sky had begun to clear. The ploughing was late this year, for the winter had been long and hard, and the snow and ice that had held it fast was only just beginning to lose its grip.

They sat under the hedge which overlooked the narrow rutted lane which separated Gregson's Farm from that of their neighbour, Will Towneley, a bluff, hearty man with a family of three sons and an aged mother who kept house for them, for he was also a widower, having buried two wives.

Jennet sat with her father and Jess, sharing their meal, and wishing it was summer, for the cold air penetrated her thin garments despite the woollen shawl which she held tightly around her, her fingers blue with the cold. She wished she had put on her thick frieze cloak and hood, which she usually wore only on her excursions to Preston Market, or to church. She glanced at her father. He looked tired, she thought, the creases around his eyes had deepened as though he were in pain, and he wore a frown. His usually ruddy face had taken on a greyish colour.

"When will you be finished?" she asked, looking at the field, only a third of which had been ploughed. The rooks and a few crows were making a great to-do over the bare, brown furrows and there were crowds of starlings and sparrows further off from the bigger birds, taking advantage of a rare feast, partaking of juicy worms turned up by the plough.

Master Gregson finished his hunk of bread and cheese, and taking up his cup of buttermilk, took a long drink. "Mayhap by noon on the morrow if we work until dark tonight and get an early start come morning. The ground is hard yet and there are many stones to be shifted, lest they harm the plough."

He pointed to a pile of stones lying further up the field. "It must be done soon, if we are to get the sowing done in time. We must pray that the weather stays fine and the wind and rain keep off for a few days."

He rose, indicating that the work must resume. Old Jess got up too, grumbling about his stiff legs. He was a taciturn old man and rarely spoke, except to complain about his "rheumatiz" or the state of the weather which affected him sorely. He pulled the layers of sacking about his spare shoulders and moved over to grasp the leading rein of Betsey, the plough horse.

He had been with the Gregson's for many years and was a distant cousin of her father's so Master Gregson kept him on even though secretly he thought Jess was getting too old for the hard work and could really only manage the lighter tasks about the farm. Today he was leading Betsey up and down the field, while John steered the plough.

Jennet rose, too, and began to collect the cups and other utensils and put them into the basket. On her way across the field she paused to stroke Betsey's velvety nose and the mare's silken neck stretched out towards her. But Jess pulled on the rein and the mare moved reluctantly away from the hedge where she had been nibbling the fresh young buds on the bushes and small trees.

Back at the farmyard Jennet found the boy Jack just coming out of the shippon, trundling a barrow-load of highly redolent cow-dung. He took it over to the dung heap in a corner of the yard where it must 'mature' before it was ready to be spread on the fields.

Jennet called out a cheery greeting to him and he answered with downcast head and a flush spreading over his homely face. She knew he adored her and had done so since he came to them as a boy of ten, some four years ago. He was called, Simple Jack, not because he was an idiot, but because he was slow of learning and had a slight stutter. His mother, a poor widow from a nearby village, had come to Master Gregson, begging for a place for him on the farm, for she was ailing and could no longer provide for him. She had died a few months later, and so Jack became a permanent member of the household. He slept among the straw in the barn, along with old Jess, and was, in his slow way, learning the work of the farm.

Jennet was fond of him, and he repaid her kindness with a dog-like devotion, often bringing her a posy of wild flowers or bright leaves or berries. He also snared the occasional rabbit or game bird which augmented their usually simple fare. Today they were having rabbit-broth, the rabbit supplied by Jack, of course. Jennet stirred the pot hanging over the fire. The broth simmered, giving off an appetising aroma. She tasted it, added a few more herbs from the bunches hanging from the beams, tasted it again and nodded with satisfaction. Then she went in to the dairy to wrap the cheeses in clean white cloths, ready to take to market the following day.

After supper that evening came the usual Bible-reading by her father. He insisted on this, no matter how tired he was. His voice, as he read from the book of Job, was not as firm as usual, but after a shaky start, he recovered and resonantly read of the trials and tribulations of the prophet and his continuing faith. They all stood round, heads bent, eyes closed, as he recited a short prayer, then paused for a moment's quiet personal contemplation.

When the "good nights" were said and Jess and Jack retired to the barn, Jennet thought it would be a good opportunity to ask her father about the stuff for the new gown.

"Father," she began hesitantly, hardly daring to ask, "could you- would it be-" she stumbled over the words.

"Well, lass, what is it? What do you want?" John asked wearily, brushing his hand over his eyes. "Can't you see I'm fair tired out, and 'tis an early start the morn if we are to get the ploughing finished?"

"I know, and I will not be a moment." She steeled herself to go on. "I just wish to ask if you can spare enough to buy a length of cloth to make a new gown. This one is in tatters and is too small now. I am ashamed to go to the market in it."

At last she had got the words out. She dared to glance at her father to see how he had taken it. His expression had not changed and he was staring abstractedly as though he had not taken her meaning.

"Oh, yes," he said at last, "it is market day tomorrow, and ye must make an early start also. Remember to milk the cows before you go. Jess can go with you, he needs the rest. I will get young Jack to help with the ploughing and hope he has sense enough to lead the horse straight. Well, good night, lass."

"But Father!" Jennet cried. "What about my gown?"

"Ah, your gown. Well, that one looks well enough to me." He turned away and she started to protest, but as he opened the door into his chamber he said, "Well, if you sell all your produce on the morrow ye may make enough for a length of sturdy cloth. But mind it's strong and will give good wear. I cannot afford to buy stuff for new gowns every few months, when there's the rent to find for Master Claythorne come Michaelmas, and there's the feed for the animals. Oh, and mind it's a seemly colour."

Jennet flew to him, so relieved was he, and flung her arms around his neck. He disengaged himself with a muttered, "Now Jenny lass, bethink thyself and act in a seemly manner." But he gave a half smile and kissed her on the brow then turned and disappeared into his room. Jennet stood staring at the closed door, completely bemused by her father's sudden and unexpected unbending.

She picked up the candle and climbed the narrow stairs with joy in her heart and almost a song on her lips. But Father would not think it 'seemly' she told herself with a smile.

Jennet undressed and got into bed quickly for the contrast between the warm kitchen and her cold bedroom was marked. She was glad she had had the foresight to put a stone bed-warmer in earlier. She snuggled down, pulling up the covers round her ears. Drifting into that delicious state between sleeping and waking, she hoped that she would have a better and more restful night than the previous one. Those dreams were disturbing. She wondered again how they could have occurred. That man - who could he be? What connection could she have with such a person? Deep inside she felt a strong conviction that she would meet him someday. But how? Where? She could find no answer to these questions and finally her tired brain gave up. Sinking into velvety blackness, she slept.

After a fairly dream-free night Jennet was up the next day while it was still dark and prepared the morning meal of oatcakes, cold sliced ham and ale before Master Gregson rose and the farmhands appeared, blinking, in the doorway, followed by Mary, panting from her run across the fields. After the milking was done and the cows sent out to pasture, the farmer took the disappointed Jack to carry on with the ploughing. Jennet changed her dress, tidied herself and took her cloak from the chest in her room.

Poor Jack, she mused. How he had wanted to go with her to market. Now she would have to put up with old Jess's alternations between sour complaints about his stiff joints and his long periods of morose silence. She was fond of the old man but he could be trying at times.

With much prompting, he helped to load the cart with her produce, then when she had assisted him to climb up to the seat, after a struggle and much complaining, Jess jerked Darby's reins and they were off.

Fortunately, the morning was fine and there was only a slight breeze but it was still cold. She and the old man huddled together under the horse blanket as the cart rattled over the stony, rutted narrow lanes towards the town. The fierce winds of previous days had dried up most of the mired ground, and they made good, if rather bumpy, progress.

Jess had relapsed into one of his silences, so Jennet had plenty of time to think. Foremost in her thoughts was how she would fashion her dress, and if she would be able to obtain the sort of material to suit both her father and herself. How she would love to have the sort of clothes she had seen fine ladies wear in the town, their silks and satins and finely-worked lace at throat and wrists. Even the gentlemen rivalled the ladies for this. She thought that they must never have to soil their hands and clothes with the sort of work she had to do. They must have many servants, she reflected with a sigh. If only she were rich!

Then she chuckled as the image of her father formed in her mind, decked out with satin and lace, with knots of ribbons below his knees, his hair in long ringlets. It seemed so ludicrous, used as she was to seeing him in plain homespun trousers and jerkin, and with his hair cut short, that she laughed out loud.

Jess, half asleep beside her, was jerked awake and looked at her askance. "I'm sorry, Jess," she muttered, trying hard to stifle her giggles, "did I disturb you? I was just thinking of something which amused me." She burst out laughing again and Jess stared at her as if she had suddenly gone mad. "Nay, lass," he grunted, looking disapprovingly at her, "but thi' feyther would not like to see thee acting so free in public."

She sobered for a moment, thinking of what her father would have said had he seen her. Then she looked at Jess. He was so muffled up in the blanket that only his eyes with their bushy grizzled brows could be seen, reminding her of a little grey mouse peering from behind a sack of meal. Uncontrollably, she fell to laughing again, and two gentlemen on horseback who were passing turned round to look. They both smiled at this pretty country girl, so merry on this cold February morning. The taller of the two doffed his plumed hat, his eyes atwinkly, and bowed in a very courtly manner.

Jennet blushed in her confusion and turned her face away from their laughing gaze. They passed on but at the bend of the lane the one who had bowed turned, rose a little in his stirrups and waved. Moving on, the two horsemen disappeared from sight.

Jennet stared after them. Something had stirred in her memory, but she could not remember quite what it was at first. Then it came to her. That man, the tall one. Something about him was vaguely familiar. But where could she have seen him before?

Was he the man in her dreams? It was not exactly the face she remembered for she had never been able to make out the features of the dream man. No, it was the way he moved when he rose to wave to her, and the set of his shoulders.

She shrugged her own shoulders in self-derision. It could not be him she told herself fiercely. This man was dressed in severely cut travelling clothes, not by any means like the satin-clothed personage, with lace adorning his coat and sleeves, who had risen to greet her in her oft-repeated dreams. It was all too ridiculous and she was a simpleton to let dreams take such a hold on her imagination.

They were now in sight of the Friargate Barrs, where they must pay a toll. This was one of the three entrances to Preston town, the other two being at the end of Fishergate and Churchgate. Friargate led directly to the Market Square, so they were almost at their journey's end.

Jennet looked ahead to see if there was any sign of the two horsemen, but in vain. They had vanished as though they were just another figment of her imagination.

With a sigh of regret which she immediately shrugged aside, she realised that she would probably never see either of them again.

CHAPTER TWO

Preston seemed busier than usual that day, with much com ing and going, not all of it market business Jennet was sure, for many riders passed them going up Friargate. They were evidently on urgent business for their horses were mud-streaked and covered with sweat, the riders drooping wearily, apparently, thought Jennet, having ridden all night.

She wondered if the gentlemen who had passed them earlier had been on the same business and what was their destination. It must be something very important, she surmised.

Their arrival at the market-place put an end to her musings. Jennet smoothed her hair and stepped down from the cart.

Because they were early they found a good place, in the corner of the market-place near to the opening into Friargate. There were many shops round the Square and on the south side stood the Town Hall, while on the north side was the fine, timber-framed house of Master Adam Morte, which had been built in 1629, only thirteen years before. There were other fine houses on that side also, but Master Morte's was the finest.

During the morning, trade was brisk and by 11 o'clock Jennet had sold more than half of her cheeses and eggs and nearly all the milk and butter.

She indulged in a little mild gossip with the housewives who gathered round her cart, most of whom knew her from her weekly appearances at the market. There were many small groups of men also, gathered round talking politics and grumbling about the taxes King Charles had lately increased. She overheard one say that Richard Shuttleworth of Gawthorpe was recruiting men for the Parliament. He was the local M.P. and was one of the fiercest opponents of the King's arbitrary methods. He had suffered a crippling law-suit shortly after he inherited his estates under James First, the present King's father, in which James had argued that in East Lancashire, those who had inherited forest lands were not the true owners, as all forests belonged to the crown.

King James's lawyers had said that the only way to settle this was for those who occupied the lands to pay extremely large fees for the deeds to be put in order. It had cost Shuttleworth and his neighbours the exorbitant sum of £11,000.

No wonder he had little cause to trust the king, for, he argued, the son was very like the father; look at the way he had enforced loans and taxed them increasingly! And his insistence on the Divine Right of Monarchs to rule as they pleased and exercise arbitrary powers, was not to be borne!

So went the talk, until one of the men hushed the speaker, a large, florid man in his fifties, and with cautious glances around, they moved off.

Jennet knew very little about politics, and did not wish to know more, but realised from things he had said, that her father was on the side of the parliament. His rent for the farm, paid annually at Michaelmas to Master Henry Claythorne, had been raised by a tenth last year, because said the steward, King Charles had levied a higher tax on his master. Her father had been understandably furious, and was hard put to it to raise the higher amount. They had had to sell one of the cows and two of their four pigs. The yield from the crops had not been good either, so no wonder he wanted to get the Long Meadow in production again.

She felt guilty at asking him for the money for the cloth for her new gown and almost decided not to buy it and to give him all the money she made, but by two o'clock when she had sold the last of the cheese and eggs and there was only a small amount of milk and butter left, she realised that she had made more than she had expected. If she was careful and got a good bargain, she could afford to buy the cloth and have a good sum left to give to her father.

Leaving the old man Jess in charge of the remaining produce, she hurried off. Looking round the various stalls which had rolls of cloth for sale she found none she liked, so decided to go to the mercers in Churchgate. Here she was lucky, the shopkeeper found a length of rich, dark green wool at the back of a shelf, only slightly faded round the edges, so she bought it after ten minutes bargaining, very cheaply. The mercer brought out some lace, thinking to tempt her into buying some for collars and cuffs, but although she would have dearly liked to succumb to the temptation, she remembered her resolve to spend as little as possible, and besides, she knew her puritan father would frown on such fripperies.

She hastened up Churchgate to get back to the Market Square and turning right into the Shambles where all the butchers shops were, she almost bumped into a handsome, middle-aged lady accompanied by a servant girl, who was carrying various parcels.

The woman stared at her as she hastily murmured an apology and suddenly took her arm, peering into her face. "It's - it's Jennet, isn't it? Why, how you've grown!"

Jennet gaped in bewilderment, surely it couldn't be - yes, it was!

"Aunt Margaret," she exclaimed, gazing delightedly at her father's sister.

"Yes, my dear, it's your Aunt Margaret," smiled the plump, well-dressed woman. "But what are you doing in Preston town? I thought John kept you chained to the farm!"

Jennet noticed the trace of bitterness in her tone, and remembered the rift that had grown between her father and aunt, when Margaret had remarried after her first husband, father's lifetime friend, had died.

She had married again only a year later, to Master Thomas Trentham, a noted Roman Catholic and Margaret had embraced that faith, too, to the undying fury and remorseless condemnation of her brother, a staunch Presbyterian. He had refused to see or speak to her again and sternly forbade his daughter to do so either.

Jennet had temporarily forgotten this ban, as aunt and niece embraced. Margaret would have had her come to her house over the bookseller's shop that her husband owned further down Churchgate, for a warming cup of mulled wine.

Jennet had to refuse politely, much as she hated doing so, for she had always been fond of Aunt Meg as a little girl, and regretted not having been able to see her for the three years since her remarriage.

She explained about Jess and the horse and wain waiting for her in the market-place and their need to get back to the farm before dark. Margaret exclaimed with surprise when she heard about her niece's frequent excursions to Preston Market, to sell her farm produce.

"How strange! You have been coming to Preston every week, and I have not seen you! But perhaps not so strange, for I rarely go to the market myself. Sarah, my maidservant, does those sort of errands for me." She indicated the little maid, standing patiently to one side, still burdened with baskets and bundles.

The child, for she could not be more than twelve, tried to sketch a curtsey, and was in great danger of dropping half of them. Jennet smiled at her thinking that this servant girl seemed to be better-dressed than she was, and she drew her cloak tighter about her, the better to hide the worn, old gown she was wearing underneath. She hoped Aunt Meg had not noticed it, but greatly feared that she had and felt ashamed. She hugged the cloth for her new gown to her, and wished that her aunt and she had not met until she was wearing it. Meg could see she was distressed and anxious to be off so she kissed her again, only remarking that her dear niece must call on her and her husband if ever she needed help, and no doubt they would meet again.

So Jennet arrived back at the market to find Jess dozing on the cart, having sold all but the tiniest trickle of milk during the hour she had been away.

On the way home, her thoughts were full of the meeting with her aunt, debating in her mind how she would break the news to her father that she had met and talked to his sister.

The fact that Margaret had married a Roman Catholic and,

indeed, become one herself, was to him the most heinous of crimes. Being a strict Presbyterian, Catholics to him were anathema as to many others of his day. The cry "No Popery!" was uttered everywhere, especially in London, where Charles First's Catholic queen was hated, with her priests and popish rituals.

Jennet felt it was a shame that her father and aunt could not be reconciled. What did it matter what religion a person was she argued to herself, as long as they did no harm to other folk and conducted their lives circumspectly, they were all Christians, after all, and worshipped the same God and if each chose to do so in a different manner, that was between themselves and their Maker. Somehow, she did not think that God, if he was the benign and merciful Creator she herself believed in, would mind very much. She knew she was going against all her father's teachings for his was a vengeful God, always ready to punish the sinner. He liked the fiery sermons of the Presbyterian Ministers, full of hellfire and damnation, but he got little of these nowadays for had not the King lately ordered that all services must abide by the Prayer Book of James the First? He called these "namby-pamby" and would have none of them, but they must still go to the Anglican church or pay a fine and while some folk were rich enough to pay the fine each week and stay away, Master Gregson and his household attended regularly but with strict instruction to pay no heed to the service. He did this because he could not afford to pay the fine, so he said. Jennet thought he was being rather simple-minded to expect them to close their ears to what was being said around them, but she dutifully tried to think of something else, not always with much success. Her father, she knew, muttered psalms throughout, and refused to join in the hymns, keeping a watchful eye on her to make sure she did not either. Jess and Jack were not affected, it all being over their heads, anyway, they not understanding very much of the parson's long-winded and barely audible sermons.

Looking ahead as they were nearing the lane leading to their farm, Jennet was surprised to see a wildly waving figure running towards them. It was the boy, Simple Jack. The cart stopped, and with his face working, and breathing in painful gasps, Jack struggled to speak. Her heart sinking with a dreadful premonition, Jennet jumped down and grasped his arms and shook him.

"What is it? What is the matter?" she demanded. "Is it father? Is he . . ?" She dared not finish, but striving to contain her impatience she waited for him to bring his voice under control. At last, he managed to speak, stumbling over the words.

"T-tis T'Maister," he spluttered, tears starting to flow. "He - he be t'taken bad." He sobbed, covering his face and moaning incoherently.

Jennet stood as if turned to stone and Jess let out a shocked, "Oh my Lord!"

Suddenly Jennet was off, running headlong down the lane, not waiting for the cart. Behind her, Jess had yelled for Jack to get on, and jerking the reins, he started the cart careering after her. Blindly she ran on, whispering, "Father! Father!" agonisingly.

Her foot caught in a pothole and she fell, sprawling. The cart stopped beside her and it was Jack who jumped out and helped her to her feet and on to the cart.

She sat, crouched, with Jack's arm around her, his own face tear-streaked as he tried to comfort her.

CHAPTER THREE

John Gregson lay unconscious in his bed, his face grey, his lips a strange bluish colour, his breath thin and rasping, a travesty of his usual self. He looked far older than his fifty-three years, as though in one short day, twenty years had come and gone, leaving the mark of old age upon him. He had lain like this since Will Towneley and his son, Richard had carried him home from where he lay in the Long Meadow, after Jack had come running in great distress to beg their help for "t'Maister", who was taken ill. Granny Towneley had followed while Henry was sent in haste for the Apothecary.

They had tried to question Jack as to what had happened but he could only stand, twisting his hands and sobbing, so they gave it up and old Granny Towneley and Will got John to bed, and tried to make him as comfortable as possible while they waited for the Apothecary. It was granny who suggested to Jack that he go and look for Mistress Jennet on her way home from market, and had sent him out with the thought that having something to do would help to calm him down.

The Apothecary, Master Phipps, was there when Jennet arrived. He had bled the sick man and shook his head when Jennet flashed a mute appeal, for her father looked so weak and frail.

"He hath suffered a suffusion of blood in the heart," he said, "and this bleeding may relieve it. But he must be kept quiet and have no alarms. I will come tomorrow to bleed him again if he hath not come to himself."

His expression was sombre as he departed, and to the eager questioning of the Towneleys, who were waiting in the kitchen with Jess and Jack, gave only a melancholy shake of the head.

Jennet sat at the bedside, holding her father's hand tightly during the rest of that day and night. She kept her eyes on his face, willing him to open his eyes and look at her, to speak her name, but they remained closed, his body unmoving. Only the faint rasp of breath told her he still lived.

The Towneleys came in to see how he fared, then went off home, promising to come the next day. Jess and Jack sat huddled in the kitchen, Jess coming in once or twice to beg her to take some food, but she would have none of it. Still later, as she sat, half frozen and dozing, she felt someone steal quietly into the room and place her cloak around her shoulders. She never noticed who it was.

Towards dawn, when Jennet had fallen asleep across the bed, she was awakened by a faint sound, like the whisper of a small sad wind among the leaves of the sycamore beside the house. But, she thought, "Tis too early in the year for the sycamore's leaves to be out. They are but the merest shimmer of green yet." She lifted her head a trifle, the better to hear. It was a voice, whispering her name, the merest thread of sound.

"Jennet," it said, "Jennet. . . ."

Joyfully, she sat up. Her father had opened his eyes, just a little, as though he was too weary to open them further and was straining to make her hear him.

"Jennet - Jennet, lass. . . ."

"Hush, father, hush now," she murmured tenderly, kissing him gently on the pale, cold cheek, "rest ye now. Do not try to speak. I am here to care for you and I'll not leave you. Ever."

"But Jenny, the field - the ploughing - t'is not finished. Must get it done. Must get . . ." and the voice trailed away, the eyes closed in utter weariness.

He slept. Jennet felt the tears stinging her eyelids, the first she had shed since her father's collapse. It must be the reaction to the strain she had been under during the long vigil. She let them fall, unheeding, striving only to stifle her sobs, lest they should awaken the sleeping man.

From the kitchen she heard subdued sounds of Jess and Jack creeping about, preparing for the new day. Then Mary's voice, raised in shocked tones, and quickly hushed. Presently, the girl came in on tip-toes, carrying a bowl of steaming broth, which Jennet accepted gratefully, suddenly realising how cold and hungry she was.

"How is t'Maister? I were reet sorry to hear he be taken bad," Mary whispered concernedly.

"He has been awake," replied her mistress, "but now he sleeps, thank God, but he is very weak. If he - when he wakens again we must try to get him to take some of this good broth. T'will help to build his strength." Mary stole out again, smiling tremulously, to impart the news to Jess and Jack, waiting eagerly in the next room.

****

During the next few weeks, John Gregson alternated between bouts of severe weakness, when he could hardly speak, and periods when he seemed almost to recover, and would demand to be allowed to get up and go on with his work about the farm. It fretted him to lie thus, waited on by Jennet and Mary, or even the men when Jennet had taken her brief periods of rest, and Mary had gone home. The Apothecary came and advocated bleeding him again, but this Jennet would not have, feeling instinctively that the taking of more blood from him would only weaken him further.

One thing puzzled her, when John had one of his brief periods of seeming recovery, he had asked particularly for Will Towneley to come and visit him privily. The Towneleys had visited to enquire of his health and Granny had sent over pots of her own preserves and calf's head broth for the invalid. Richard Towneley had even, with Jess's help, finished off the ploughing of the Long Meadow, when Jennet had told them how her father had fretted at its not being finished. Will had also promised to see to the sowing of the oats and barley. Jennet was glad of his and his son's help, for, being able to report this to John eased his mind, she felt.

But she knew also, that it secretly irked the fiercely independent man to have to accept such charity.

Will was with her father now, and this was the second of his visits. She wondered what could be the meaning of it. That it was a business matter she was sure. But what business could her father have with Will Towneley, when they had never been close friends and hardly exchanged more than a dozen words in a year? Still, they had proved their neighbourliness, with the offers of help and little acts of kindness, for which she for one, was duly grateful.

It was at the end of April, on a day new-washed with early morning showers and the sun shining with welcome warmth, when Will Towneley arrived at the farm gate with his son, Richard, and another soberly dressed man who looked as though he might be a parson - or a lawyer?

Jennet was with her father when a flustered Mary ushered them in. Will introduced the strange man as "Master Wilson from Preston," who had come at his request to conduct their business. He was a lawyer - "of great repute," said Will. Richard Towneley stood awkwardly, his face flushed, hat in hand, looking at the floor. Jennet rose, wondering what this was all about, and with a feeling of dread of what she knew not, made to leave the room, assuming that this was men's business, and as a female, she was not wanted. Will, however, put his large, red hand on her arm and stopped her.

"Nay, Mistress Jennet, there's no cause for you to go, this concerns you also." He motioned for her to resume her seat.

Feeling utterly bewildered and not a little apprehensive, she did so.

Her father was sitting propped up with pillows and looking frailer than ever. His face had grown thinner and his cheeks were sunken. She wished Will Towneley had not brought his son and this stranger. She was sure her father was in no fit state to receive visitors, and wondered what could be the purpose, and why did it concern her?

The lawyer had taken some papers from a large bag and putting them in order, cleared his throat. Will Towneley looked solemn, and Richard, acutely embarrassed, as though he was wishing he was anywhere else but here.

"Now, sirs - and the young mistress," began Master Wilson, coughing apologetically and with a slight bow towards Jennet, "we are here this day to conduct the preliminary business, as you are no doubt all aware, of the betrothal of Richard Thomas Towneley, bachelor, of Whitegate Farm, Broughton, near Preston in Amounderness, to Jennet Gregson, Spinster, of Gregson's Farm in the same locality."

The lawyer's voice droned on, speaking in dry, ponderous tones, uttering legalities, which Jennet never heard. She felt as though dark waters were closing over her head. She was drowning, unable to breathe. With a great effort, she clawed her way to the surface, and darted a quick questioning look at her father. He returned her look, his eyes mutely appealing, and gave her hand a weak squeeze as if begging her to understand.

She dropped her gaze, her thoughts in a turmoil. She, betrothed to Richard Towneley! It was impossible. She had never even thought of him in that way. True, she had known him most of her life, but never intimately. So, she could not say she really *knew* him.

She had had her dreams, of course, all young girls do, but Richard Towneley did not figure in any of them. Irrelevantly, there came into her mind a memory of the dream she'd had of the rich room and the shadowy figure at the table, whose face she had never seen. Or had she? But that was not for Jennet Gregson, the daughter of a poor tenant farmer.

She stole a glance at Richard. He had been staring at her, but looked away quickly, unable to meet her eyes. He was a tallish, slim youth with sandy, unruly hair, cut short, and a pleasant, open face. He was about twenty years old, the middle son of Master Towneley. His elder brother, William, was already betrothed, at twenty-three, and the younger one, Henry, was but a lad of fifteen. So, they had picked Richard, she thought, as being the most suitable. She did not find out until much later that when John had spoken with Will Towneley, in one of his private talks to that individual, he had discussed Jennet's future and told Will that he was worried about her being left alone when he passed on. Will had mentioned the idea of marrying her to someone who could look after her, and in fact, had proposed himself as Jennet's husband-to-be. But John, weak as he was, would have none of this. His Jennet, married to a man nearly as old as himself, and who had buried two wives already! It was unthinkable.

So they had settled on Richard as being the most eligible and Richard himself was not averse to the idea. He had long admired pretty Jennet from afar, covertly watching her each Sunday when she appeared at Church with her father and the two farm-hands. As he stood there in John Gregson's chamber, he was secretly elated, seeing at last the fulfilment of his dreams. But it was a pity they had not thought fit to acquaint the maid with their intentions; he would have liked to have been able to court her first, and hoped she would not be put off by having it sprung so suddenly upon her. But the old man, her father, had wanted it done quickly and it was plain to see why. He had not long to live and knew it and wished to see his daughter settled before he died.

Master Wilson had finished speaking and, with his dry cough, turned to Will, and indicating a place on the document he proffered, desired him to sign his name. Will couldn't read, but he could sign his name and so could Richard. Then it was John's turn and he was held up by Master Wilson and Will while he signed, his hand shaking. Then the lawyer turned to Jennet but she, feeling trapped, made a last protest.

"Father!" she exclaimed. "Why do I have to do this? I have not been told of it, and in truth, I have no wish to marry yet. Saving your presence, Sir."

She curtsied to Richard, who, seeing his hopes in danger of being dashed, coloured up and went towards her, but was stopped by his father.

"Nay, lass, be not upset. This is done at your father's earnest wish," Will said. "We are all most anxious for your welfare, and my dear son Richard, is, and has been for a long while, your most devoted admirer. He has confided in me ofttimes how he wished to be your sweetheart, but your youth and your father's need of you were deemed enough reasons for leaving it until you were older. Now that circumstances have changed . . ." he paused, glancing towards John, who, trying to sit up, had exhausted himself, and fallen back on the pillows.

He beckoned to Will, who bent over, and John whispered to him to beg the others to wait in the other room while he had words with his daughter. They went out, Richard casting a despairing look back at Jennet, and Master Wilson muttering, "This is most irregular, most irregular. I have never heard of such a thing."

Alone with her father, Jennet threw herself on the bed, clasping her arms about his neck. "Father, dear Father, why must this be?" she wailed. "I want only to stay with you, do not send me away, why did you not tell me? Must I wed this man who is almost a stranger to me?" She sobbed in despair.

"My Jennet, do not think I have not thought on this long and earnestly. I had no wish to part with my only child, but you know, you must marry some time, sooner or later. A young defenceless maid needs a husband to protect her, especially now, in these unsettled times, and sooner it must be for I will not be here to guard you much longer."

"No, father, do not say it!" she cried. "You will not die. You *must* not die, I could not bear it."

"But you must know it is the truth. I cannot last much longer and my earnest wish is to see you safely married ere I go. Promise me that you will accept this betrothal with a good heart. Will Towneley is a good man and of our faith, and his son, Richard is also, and loves you dearly as he has sworn to me. After you are married, Richard shall live here and look after the farm, so you will not be going away and he has promised that Jess and Jack shall not want for a home. So come now, my girl, give your promise and please your father on his dying bed."

Jennet dried her tears. "Very well, father, if it is your wish," she said quietly and going to the door, she opened it and summoned the three men back in to the room.

"I will sign now," she said, and did so. Richard's face was wreathed in smiles and taking her hand he kissed it fervently. "I promise you, my betrothed, you will not regret this."

His father came over and kissed her heartily on the cheek and Lawyer Wilson shook her hand, obviously much relieved that the business had been concluded satisfactorily. Will insisted that they should all drink a health to the newly affianced pair, with the bottle of wine he had had the foresight to bring, knowing there would not be such a thing in John Gregson's house.

John lay back on his pillows, when Jennet hastened in to him after they had gone. "I have a great content in me," he said to her, "but I cannot truly rest until you are really married."

And so, a bare three weeks later, on a fair and shining morning in May, Richard and Jennet were wed in Broughton Church. Will stood in for her father and William, whose own wedding to Alice Farnworth, the miller's daughter from Goosnargh, was only weeks away, was Richard's best man.

The wedding was conducted quietly, with only their own families present and there was no celebration, only the cold collation provided by Granny Towneley, at Whitegate Farm, after the ceremony.

Then the bride and groom were conducted by their relatives back to Jennet's own home and left there to begin their married life. John Gregson received them with tears in his eyes, and kissed them both.

Jess and Jack, with young Mary, stood waiting to offer their good wishes. Poor Jack, his young heart broken, wept unashamedly, but brightened up when Richard pressed a shilling onto each of them and bade them go to his father's house where they were invited to supper.

And Master Gregson, lying on his narrow bed, smiled and said, "*Now* I am really content."

A few days later, John passed away quietly in his sleep, leaving a country poised on the brink of Civil War, and while the storm clouds gathered, a young bride and her husband began their life together, little dreaming what lay in store, both for themselves and for King and Country.

CHAPTER FOUR

Richard proved a kind and understanding husband and for the first few days of their marriage when she was still feeling shy and uncomfortable with this man who was almost a stranger to her, he courted her as he had wished to do all along, bringing her little gifts and treating her with a gentleness and courtesy which completely disarmed her.

If it were not for the anxiety she had felt for her father and then her grief over his death, these would have been idyllic days. Even then, she found comfort in his nearness and strength and often, when grief overcame her, she would instinctively turn to him, and find his strong arms about her while she sobbed unrestrainedly on his shoulder.

And so the days went on, and they were in June, a month Jennet had always loved, with its long sunny days filled with the song of birds. The Sycamore tree at the side of the house was now in full foliage and Jennet liked to sit in its leafy shade. She was there now, shelling peas for their main meal that evening. Every now and then, her hands would lie idle while her mind reviewed the events of the past few months and the changes that had taken place. Richard was now the tenant of the farm, the transfer having been arranged with Master Claythorne, who managed these lands for Sir Gilbert Hoghton, of Hoghton Tower.

Mary was now a full time member of the household. She had turned fourteen in April and Richard had prevailed upon her mother - who already had a large family to provide for and needed the money - to allow her daughter to live at the farm for a higher wage. Richard felt that Jennet needed more help in the house and dairy. Jennet no longer milked the cows; that task had become Jack's, with occasional help from Jess. The old man, who was now over seventy, was more of a liability than a help, Richard thought, but because of the promise they had made to Jennet's father and also because neither of them would have cared to turn him off to fend for himself, they allowed him to take things easily and turn his hand, if he cared to, to do any odd jobs which were within his capabilities. At his age he could not expect to live much longer, although, with his sturdy yeoman stock, he could live until he was eighty, and probably would, Richard thought ruefully. He had no other relatives, apart from John and his daughter, and they were but distantly related. He had been married but his wife had died many years before he came to live with them and they'd had no children. So with Jess unable to do much and Jack looking after the cows and the shippon, Richard was looking out for a farm-hand to help with the heavy work. He had discussed this with Jennet the evening before. This was something which Jennet found greatly to her liking, the fact that her husband thought he should talk things over with his wife, which her father had never done with her, and most probably, even with her mother. It gave her the feeling of being truly the mistress.

"Jennet, my love," he asked, "what do you think of Seth Blackley, from the village?"

"Seth Blackley?" Jennet looked up from her sewing. "What about him?"

"I am thinking of asking him to come over during the day to help with the bottom field. The ditch needs clearing out and the hedges trimming and then if he should prove a good worker, I thought we might take him on permanently."

"Well, you seem to have made up your mind already," Jennet remarked, feeling secretly very pleased that he was troubling to discuss it with her, "but if you are asking for my opinion, I would say why not Harry Baines, who has lately lost his father and has an old mother to keep? He has worked for your father at various times and you should know what sort of a worker he is. Seth Blackley is a surly man and not, to my mind, anxious to work hard."

"You may be right," smiled her husband. "I remember Harry;

he is a strong lad and willing, and since he has started courting Alison Starkie, he will be anxious to find permanent work. My father would have taken him on, but for the fact that he had three willing workers in William, Henry and me, as well as the farm-hands, Joseph and Tom."

"Then you had better engage him right away, for Master Towneley has lost one of his workers when Master Richard got married and he will be looking for a good man to replace him."

Jennet smiled to herself as she remembered how they had laughed over her sally. Yes, it was good to be able to laugh and share a joke. She was beginning to expand like a flower opening its petals to the sun. She still missed her father and sorrowed over his loss, but life had to go on, and she had to admit, it promised to be much more pleasant than she had dreamed.

That evening at supper, Richard was pensive.

"What is troubling you?" she asked as she served him his meat. "Is the mutton not to your liking?"

"Nay, my love, it is excellent. You are a very fair cook and these peas are delicious."

"Then what is it? This is the first time I have seen you so glum. Something must have displeased you."

"Nothing on this farm, but 'tis the news I received from my father when I saw him in the bottom field this morning. He came across to acquaint me with it and in truth it is disturbing, though I cannot say it is unexpected."

Jennet looked at him in alarm and started to speak, but he went on, "It is this trouble 'twixt the King and Parliament. It seems there will be no resolving it. You may have heard that many gentlemen have been recruiting men to make a stand, some are for the King and some are for Parliament."

Jennet remembered the talk she had heard in Preston market place and the gentlemen she had seen riding post-haste into the town. There had been many such on the subsequent visits she had made and she had noticed an air of disquiet. People talked in groups, keeping their voices low as if they feared to be overheard.

"But Richard, will this affect us?" she enquired with uneasy dread.

"I fear it may, for I have heard that Lord Strange, the Earl of Derby's son, has called a great meeting upon Preston Moor, which is not far from us, of all those loyal to the King, and 'tis certain that they will call to arms all the able-bodied men of this locality. Indeed, I have heard rumours of men being pressed into service, whether they would or no. I have no wish to serve with those who are acknowledged Papists. I, with my father, and yours also, have always been in favour of Parliament and the Protestant religion. King Charles is keeping a stranglehold on this country and will not listen to reasonable men. He has, as you know, already dissolved the Parliament out of hand because they would not listen to his demands, only two years ago." Richard paused, his eyes sombre.

"Do you think, then, that these King's men, these - Royalists, is it - may wish to force you to serve with them against all your principles?" Jennet asked with a sinking feeling in her stomach. She had no wish for Richard to leave her just as she was beginning to delight in his company.

"They may indeed, and so I would rather, if the situation is not improved, seek service with Master Richard Shuttleworth of Gawthorpe, or even Alexander Rigby, who is the Member of Parliament for Wigan. They are both in the vicinity, with the object of recruiting men in Parliament's cause."

"Oh, Richard, what are we to do?" The tears started in Jennet's eyes as she contemplated the disruption of all their lives. Even old Jess and Jack had paused in their eating at Richard's portentous announcement, while Mary had started up with a wail and knelt at Jennet's side, catching her mistress's hand.

"Oh, Mistress, Mistress!" she cried. "What be a-gooing to happen to us? 'Tis a reet shame, a reet shame, an' no mistake!"

"Now, Mary, control yourself. Everything will be alright, just you wait and see." Jennet unclasped the girl's hand and, turning to Richard, asked tremblingly, but with a great effort to remain calm, "W-when will you have to go?"

"Oh, not for a while, I should think. When I am certain that there is going to be a conflict, perhaps, or there is a certainty that the King's men will be coming here to recruit. In that case, we must keep a watch and if there is a danger of it I must make arrangements to be off at a moment's notice."

"I will g-go wi' thee, Master Richard," cried Jack eagerly. "I will g-go and h-help to fight the King!"

"Nay, Lad," laughed his master, "there will be no call for you to go. You are a trifle young yet and anyway, I must leave you behind to take care of your mistress, she will have need of you and Jess then. And who says I may have to go yet? Let us only be prepared, just in case."

Old Jess grunted in repudiation of the idea of Jack's looking after anyone and finished off his ale.

"Young Jack-a-napes," he muttered, "gets above himself, he do. He'd run a mile at the sight of a musket!"

"N-nay, I wouldn't," spluttered Jack.

Richard and Jennet laughed at the two as they argued, the difference between them being so marked, but their laughter was partly a reaction to the uneasy feelings which beset them.

Despite their fears, the next few weeks went by without further alarms, though there were rumours of this or that gentleman ranging the district recruiting men for one side or the other.

What did begin to claim their attention was something entirely different and much more pleasant.

Sixteen-forty-two was the year in which the Preston Guild Merchant was due to be held, which occurred every twenty years. Preston had been granted a charter by Henry II in 1179, which constituted the town as a free borough. It was the subject of great pride among the townsfolk and they celebrated it with much rejoicing. Some claimed that there had been an even earlier charter granted by Henry I, but there was no record of this, so it could not be proved.

The townsfolk were, by the charter, granted certain privileges and advantages not enjoyed by many other towns, such as the right to trade anywhere in the realm and to hold a Guild Merchant. In subsequent charters, confirmed by various monarchs, they were also given the right to take wood from the royal forest of Fulwood for their house-building and deadwood for their fires and for this purpose also, peat turves from Preston Moor.

Records from the earliest Guild Merchants were known, with the names of burgesses then enrolled. It was the custom also, for already sworn burgesses to enrol their sons at each succeeding Guild. For various reasons the Guild was not held regularly during those early years, notably the burning and sacking of the town by Robert Bruce in 1322, and during the Wars of the Roses. But since 1542, it had been held every twenty years.

Whether it would be held in 1642 had been in some doubt by the people. The county was in such a state of unrest that they thought it would be unwise. So the surprise was great when it was announced by Edmund Werden, the Mayor, that it would take place as usual. The preparations had already begun. Great quantities of ale and wine and foodstuffs were ordered for the banquets to be attended by the noble families and local gentry, and plays, masques and concerts arranged for their entertainment.

For the common people there would be fairs, morris dancing, mummers, bear-baiting, cock fighting, wrestling matches and the like which the ordinary townsfolk delighted in. It was to be a week of festivity and all the local Guilds in their various liveries and with their banners held aloft, would walk in procession through the town. It would start on the 29th August this year and usually finished with a grand torchlight procession through all the main streets.

Jennet felt very excited at the thought of it and hoped she would be able to see at least some of the sights.

Richard was sceptical about the whole thing and thought the town council was being unrealistic in holding the Guild Merchant at such a time,

"Oh, no," Jennet argued with him, "I think it will be something to look forward to. The common people have such hard, dull lives and with these anxious times added to their troubles, they will be glad indeed to have these festivities to brighten up their existence."

"But what about the great lords and their ladies, they don't need more banquets and balls to brighten up their existence and think of the money the council is spending on them. To my mind, they could put it to better use fortifying the town against the time when it is needed - or, let them use for the benefit of the 'common people', as your ladyship calls them." He bowed in mock courtesy and taking her hand kissed it with exaggerated gallantry.

"Your servant, Ma'am," he spoke in mincing tones and pirouetted round the room, with many flourishes of an imaginary courtier's feathered hat.

"You are a buffoon, Richard," Jennet, laughing until the tears came, collapsed on to a stool. She composed herself after a while and thought how much of a boy he still was, even at twenty-one years old. A boy - and a man too, and she was glad of it. Sobering, she hoped that his manhood would not be taxed too much in any forthcoming events. She prayed that these events would not happen but greatly feared that nothing would stop them. She would not say or think the words, but what she meant was war or conflict in any form, and, there was something else on her mind.

Rising, she curtsied, and advancing primly towards him said, "Well my Lord Richard, does your lordship fancy this is seemly conduct for the father of a forthcoming family! T'would seem, my Lord, that a more sober mien would better become you."

Richard was smiling as she first advanced, then staring, his expression changing from utter disbelief to amazed delight.

He swept her off her feet, hugging her and covering her face with kisses. She protested, but he held her fast.

"My love! Can it be true? You are sure?"

Gently but firmly, she disengaged herself. "Yes, I am sure, and it is well that Jess and Jack and Mary are engaged elsewhere, for I would not care to have them witness such unseemly conduct." The smile on her face belied her words.

Jess and Jack were, at the time, 'engaged' in the afternoon's milking, and Mary had begged a few hours off to go and see her mother and brothers and sisters.

Richard laughed and said, "But I would not care if they did, are we not wed? And since when was it unseemly for husband and wife to show their love? As for this 'forthcoming family' - what a quaint turn of phrase you have, my love - I would like to shout the news throughout the whole county of Lancashire, nay, the whole of England, so happy am I!"

"Nay, Richard, we must not spread the news yet. I am but two months gone, so we must wait until a more appropriate time."

"Appropriate time! And when is that to be? You mean when your are waddling around with a belly as big as a house? When is my son to be born?"

"Hush, Richard," she chided, "do not be so uncouth, and what if it chances to be a daughter? As to its birth-time..." she counted swiftly on her fingers, "about February, I think. I will consult Mistress Thomson about it and ask her to attend my lying-in."

Mistress Thomson, or Goodwife Thomson as she was generally known, was the midwife, who lived in a tiny cottage on the outskirts of Broughton Village and was available to help with sickness and the laying out of those lately dead.

"Well," said Richard, "I confess I would rather it were a son, but if 'tis a girl-child, then I shall be happy too, for she is sure to be like her sweet mother."

He kissed his young wife ardently and she returned it in good measure, then pushed him away with a smile. "This will not get us forward with our supper. Jess and Jack will be here anon, clamouring for their meat."

So she busied herself about the stone-floored kitchen, preparing the meal and setting the table, while Richard sat and watched her fondly.

Now they were in the second week of August and the weather had turned sultry, with clouded skies. Richard gazed anxiously at the sky. He'd hoped for a few more weeks of sunshine to ripen the crops so they would have a good harvest come September.

After a heavy thunderstorm on the Saturday, during which he had stood at the kitchen-door railing against the weather, for such heavy rain could ruin the crop, the sky cleared and the sun shone once more. He was relieved and thankful, Jennet knew, for he had set great store at making a success of this, his first venture as his own master.

About a week before Preston Guild Merchant was due to begin, Jennet was surprised to receive a letter by the carrier on one of his usual visits. No one had ever sent her a letter before. She turned it over and over, but there was no clue as to its sender, only her name and address and the seal which bore a strange device embossed upon it. She could not make it out properly but thought it looked like an animal of some kind standing on its hind legs. Whoever had sent it knew she was married for it was addressed to "Mistress Jennet Towneley."

"Well," she said to herself, "I will not find out who has sent it unless I open it." So, in some trepidation, she found a knife and slit open the paper. It was written in a neat, careful hand and started, "My dear niece, Jennet." Swiftly, she turned to the last page and saw the signature, "Your affectionate Aunt Meg."

So it was from Aunt Margaret! She thought with a sense of guilt that they should have sent her aunt the news of her father's death and her own altered status, but there had been at the time such a state of confusion and anxiety that she had not thought of it. Nor had she been able to tell her father of her meeting with her aunt, fearing to upset him in his frail state. Later, she had told Richard of it, and wondered if she should inform her aunt, but Richard, being of the same persuasion as her father, had said firmly that she should respect her father's wishes about not having anything to do with Margaret, and he himself desired that his wife should not become involved with Papists. So she left it at that, but secretly thought that they were being unkind and that men could be very obstinate and stubborn in their opinions, especially when it came to their religion or politics.

So, wondering, she read the letter and learned that Aunt Meg knew of these events.

"My dear niece, Jennet," it read. "It is with great sorrow that I write to you, having lately learned of my brother John's death. I must also offer you my condolences, for I know how you loved and respected your father, despite his often harsh and rigid ways. He was a good man, withal, and despite the unforgiving way he treated me, I still loved him well, for he was my only brother, nay, my only kin, apart from your dear self. My informant, should you be wondering, was Mistress Thomson, whom I met on one of her rare visits to the town. She, being the great gossip she is, could not wait to tell me the news, for such is her way, liking well to be first to spread news, be it good or bad. I knew her well when I was younger and living at home. It seems also that I must offer you my felicitations, for she spoke of your marriage and the forthcoming birth of your child. I and my husband send, therefore, our good wishes to yourself and your husband and would prevail upon you both, if you should be in Preston during the coming Guild week, to call upon us and partake of a glass of wine and some refreshment."

"So, it was the midwife," mused Jennet. "I might have known, she *is* a great gossip and probably the news of my pregnancy will be all over the village by now, so there is no point in keeping it a secret. And what of Aunt Margaret? I would dearly love to see her again and resolve the difference between our two households. I must consult Richard about this although I fear her will be as stubborn as my father. . . ."

When Richard came in she showed him the letter. His reading was better since he'd had Jennet to coach him, so he managed to read it, stumbling over the bigger words. When he finished, his face was non-committal.

"What shall I do?" she beseeched him. "Shall I answer it? Or do we ignore it, forgetting she is my own kin? What does it matter whether she be Papist or Puritan, Anglican - or even Jew? How can you be such a bigot, as my father was and your father is too?"

He stared at her, amazed at her outburst, then turned away. "Well Richard, what is it to be?" she demanded.

"I must think about it," he answered slowly. "I must think about what is best. You cannot expect me to change the outlook I have had all my life, in an instant."

So with that she had to be content for the time being, but she determined not to let the matter rest. That night in their bedchamber, which used to be her father's - Mary now had the use of Jennet's old room - she judged the time to be right to press the matter further. She was very cunning about it, waiting until Richard was relaxed and drowsy after a particularly passionate bout of love-making. She had been submissive and loving all the evening, then when they had retired she had thrown herself into their love-making with a fire that surprised even herself. Now, with his arm about her, half asleep, she roused him slightly by saying, very softly, "Richard, my dear husband, may I ask if you have thought more about the letter Aunt Meg sent? Please say I may reply and, please, please, let us accept her invitation. I want it so much, it tears my heart for us to be at odds with my own dear aunt."

Richard sat up suddenly. Jennet, who had been leaning over while she spoke, and was about to shed a few tears on to his naked chest - and not all those tears were affected - was thrown sideways, clutching at the bed-cover to stop herself falling out of bed.

He turned to regard her, then spoke slowly and deliberately. "Jennet, my dear wife, my only love, you are the most cunning, the most devious maid I have ever known. So that is why you were so loving. It was all a pretence to get your own way." He glared at her and she quailed, then took his hand, while the tears which were already in her eyes spilled over.

"Oh, do not be angry, I confess I sought to win your approval so you might look on my request with favour, but it was not a pretence, my loving you, for I do with all my heart and - and I am not a maid, but your wife and the mother-to-be of your child."

"Do not weep, love. Dry your tears and I will try to think of a good solution to your problem, but I cannot bring my thoughts into order while you are in distress. Come now, it is late and we must soon sleep."

Making an effort, Jennet stifled her sobs and, drying her eyes on the counterpane, looked at her husband inquiringly. He was silent for a few moments, thinking hard, while she held his hand tightly. At last he spoke.

"I have been thinking about this matter all evening and had not quite made up my mind when we retired, so I decided to sleep on it and acquaint you with my decision on the morrow. But now you have forced me to make it sooner and I cannot be pleased about that. You know my feelings on the matter of Papists and I cannot change my opinion so easily. To me, as to both our fathers, as you have said, they are as a plague, to be shunned, wherever they show themselves. But, I dare say, there are good and bad among them as there are among those of any other persuasion, even our own." He smiled deprecatingly, then went on.

"I know how much you wish to renew acquaintance with your aunt, but you must remember that I cannot afford to become involved with any of their faith. You know that they are, to a man, pledged to fight for the King. Oh, yes. I know that the King himself is not a Papist, and his main followers are Anglicans. Indeed, I am not against the King, and would swear fealty to him any day, if he would cease his absurd demands and bow to Parliament's desires, all would be well. But we know he will not, and so I am for the Parliament. But I wander from our own affairs, and so I have decided —" he paused, teasing her, and she prodded him, urging him to go on.

"Well my love - I think - I think you should write a letter to your aunt, with a word of thanks for her good wishes, and say also that if your are in Preston next week - which you may well be - and you should happen to meet her, you may exchange greetings and that is as far as I will go."

It was not all she had wished for, but it was something. So she thanked him and kissed him tenderly. Soon he was fast asleep beside her, but she lay for a long time, planning how to write the letter she would send to Aunt Meg.

CHAPTER FIVE

It was the day when Preston Guild week was to start, 29th August 1642. Jennet and Richard were setting out on their day's excursion. Will Towneley had lent them his pony and trap for the day and Jennet felt as proud as a queen to be riding in it, used as she was to their own cumbersome farm wagon.

She still wore black for her father, the gown bought for her by Richard, but it fitted her well and she had embellished it with snowy collar and cuffs of linen, with a tiny edging of lace.

The cloth for her green dress still lay at the bottom of her chest. She had never had the time nor the inclination to sew it during the weeks of her father's illness. After his death she could not wear it so she put it away with the memories of that day.

Now her life was filled with Richard and her coming child. She was not showing her pregnancy yet, she thought thankfully. At her throat was a silver brooch, Richard's wedding gift, and on her hair, now coiled up and held with pins was a new, white coif. Altogether, she thought, looking at herself in the bottom of a much burnished copper pan, she looked a well set-up young matron.

To Richard, gazing at her with admiration and love, she was beautiful, with starry eyes and pink-flushed cheeks, with the excitement of anticipation. He was as proud of her as she was, to be riding in this smart and elegant way on a wonderful day out with a handsome husband at her side.

He helped her up gallantly on to the leather covered seat, clicked his teeth at the pony, jerked the reins and they were moving towards the gate. The cheers and good wishes of those left behind followed them.

The others, of course, were not to be done out of their share of the week's festivities. Richard, never a hard master, though he could be firm when he chose, had decided that although he could not spare all of them to be away from their work at once, they could each have a day off during the week to go to Preston. Jess didn't really want to go. He didn't fancy walking round Preston all day with *his* legs and anyway, he'd seen several Guilds already in his lifetime, so he planned to sit in the sun, if it stayed fine, with his old clay pipe, or maybe potter round the little garden. He might even give a hand to Jack and Harry if they needed it.

Richard had taken on Harry Baines as Jennet had suggested and he had proved an able and willing worker. He didn't live at the farm but came in every day from the village. He was going to the guild on the next day with Alison, his sweetheart.

Mary was going with Jack on the day following, along with her brothers and sisters, those who were old enough to go. Her mother had to stay at home to look after the younger ones. Mary wished her mother could go too, but she was thankful to be able to take some of them off that work-worn and weary woman's shoulders, even if only for a day, and had promised to give her mother a full and detailed account of the day's happenings when they returned.

As they neared the town, Jennet saw that there were many other vehicles and riders on horseback, converging towards the Friargate Bars at the northern approach to the town.

Some of the coaches were grand affairs, elegantly gilded and embellished with their owner's badges and coats of arms; obviously their occupants were grand personages indeed. There were also many vehicles of the humbler sort, farm carts and wains, light carts with ponies such as their own, horses of every size and variety, such as the huge shire horse carrying a family of parents and three small children. Some rode on donkeys and there were countless people on foot. All seemed in festive mood, calling out greetings to those they were acquainted with, there was much laughter and many ribald comments from the younger bachelors as they eyed the pretty young maids who, blushing, hid their faces, but peeped out between their fingers with scarcely concealed smiles.

It was a beautiful day, and very warm, the sky overhead a deep, intense blue, with a few clouds like puffs of white foam, but there were some greyish clouds banked at the horizon.

Jennet was glad she had thought to fetch her cloak, now neatly folded on the seat beside her, in case it should rain before the day was out. She hoped it would not, for nothing must spoil this wonderful day. On the floor at their feet was the covered basket with their lunch for they would be sure to need refreshment and Richard did not care to take his wife to an inn or tavern for these, frequented as they sometimes were by rough and uncouth characters.

Walking up Friargate after they had stabled the pony and trap, Jennet with her cloak over her arm and Richard carrying the basket, they found that nearly all shops and places of business were closed and shuttered. The inns and taverns were doing good business, as was evinced by the sound of laughter and singing emanating from their open doors.

In the market-place they stopped to watch a bear-baiting, but this was not to Jennet's liking, her sympathies were all with the poor, chained, shambling bear, looking rough and ill-kept with many scars upon its hide. It was growling and striking out with huge paws at the pack of mangy dogs ranging round it, darting and snapping and snarling. She turned away, feeling sick at heart, and Richard put his arm around her. Next, their attention was drawn to a group of mummers, and here Jennet forgot the bear, for she was enthralled by their enactment of a Mystery Play. It was St. George and the Dragon, which Jennet had never seen before. When it was ended, they crossed the square with its High Cross, to the opening into Church-gate and thence to the Parish Church. Here they waited among the large crowd which was already there. They did not wait long. Soon, the church doors opened and there emerged the Guild Mayor, Master Edmund Werden, with his Guild officials attendant about him, Bailiffs, Stewards and Aldermen, resplendent in their furred robes. They had been attending Divine Service.

The Guild Mayor, with his heavy gold chain of office and carrying his rod of authority, moved down the church steps to the cheers of the assembled townsfolk. He and his retinue were followed by the nobility and gentry, whose rich and splendid attire made Jennet gasp with admiration. Here were silks, satins and rich velvets in the very latest London fashions, in every conceivable shade and jewels sparkled about their persons.

Jennet stared open-mouthed, clinging to her husband's arm, jostled by the crowd, whose oohs and aahs and other cries of admiration mingled with cheering, rang in their ears. A band struck up a martial air joining in the procession which was to march through all the main streets of the town. They would be joined by all the companies of Trades, each in its own livery and carrying its own banner.

First to the Churchgate Bars, where a scholar from the local school would read a speech, then a hogshead of ale would be broached and a glass offered to the Mayor to drink the health, first of the King, then the Queen. After the nobility and the rest had drunk, the residue was given to the townsfolk. This happened both at the Fishergate Bars and then at the Friargate Bars, from when they proceeded back up Friargate to the Market Cross, where the company divided. The Mayor, Council and Burgesses both of noble and lesser rank, went to the Guild Hall for the Mayoral luncheon, and the companies of trades each to their separate Halls for their own repast.

Feeling in need of refreshment themselves, and Jennet hot and tired from all the walking about and the excitement, they sat on the lower steps of the Market Cross and began to eat their lunch. Jennet had packed mutton pasties, bread, butter and cheese, a tart made from apples, cinnamon and cream, and jugs of ale and milk.

They ate and drank in companionable silence, Jennet feeling still bemused by all she had seen, but gloriously happy.

She would not have missed this for the world, she thought. Richard, drinking his ale, watched her. He was glad he had brought her, she had so loved the pageantry and colour and there had been little enough of that in her young life. They sat for a while, until Jennet felt more rested and refreshed. There were not many people about now, most had departed to partake of their own midday meal, though there were a few country folk like themselves, resting and eating in various parts of the market-place.

Then a band of Morris Men appeared and Jennet sprang up at once, hastily bundling the remains of the meal into the basket. The crowds began to gather and Jennet noticed that the upper windows of the houses and shops round the square were filled with people enjoying a comfortable vantage point from which to watch the proceedings. She supposed there had been many watching like this during the morning, when the Mayor's procession had taken place, although she had not really noticed, being so engrossed in everything herself.

How lovely it would be, she thought, to have a house in the town and be able to see everything from the comfort of your own home. Probably Aunt Margaret and her husband had been watching too.

The Morris Men, accompanied by fife and drum, began their performance, weaving their intricate patterns, with much slapping of sides and buttocks and waving of kerchiefs, and the tinkling of the bells attached to their sturdy legs took up all her attention.

They watched the races, the tug of war, the little plays performed by the school-children, with which Jennet was enchanted, laughed at the antics of a troupe of clowns, marvelled at the skill and dexterity of the jugglers. Richard bought her a bunch of gay ribbons and a curiously wrought comfit box from an old, wrinkled, dark gypsy woman who wanted to tell her fortune, but Jennet refused, feeling a sudden, queer shudder of apprehension for which she couldn't account, run through her. She turned away, groping for Richard's hand. The bells rang out from the tower of the Parish Church proclaiming the hour of four in the afternoon. Richard decided it was time to go home.

"Come on, love," he whispered, "you are fatigued, and it grows late. Let us go, for I fear it may soon rain." She glanced up at the sky and was surprised to see how the clouds had gathered. They made their way as fast as they were able through the crowds, who still milled about the streets, to where they had left the pony and cart, and were soon on their way home.

Jennet put on her cloak and hood and Richard his jerkin, for the first few drops of rain had begun to fall. Jennet leaned against Richard's shoulder, half asleep, recalling the day's events, and wishing she wouldn't have to wait another twenty years to witness such splendours again. She thought it odd that she hadn't seen anything of her aunt and wished there had been an opportunity for them to meet again. She was too tired and sleepy to think much on the subject, however, and nodded off while the cart rattled over the stones, the pony's hooves beating a rhythm in time with the now swiftly falling rain.

September came in with rain and then it brightened again. Richard and his small band of workers were harvesting the crop of barley, oats and corn.

He had had offers of help from his father and brothers, if he should not be finished by the time their own harvesting was over but he hoped to have it finished before that. Whitegate Farm was larger than his, with several more fields and although his father had more men to help him, Richard did not feel they could finish so soon. The weather had been unsettled for some weeks and these were the first few fine days since the Guild. So he hoped he could get it done before the weather deteriorated again. He had another reason for wishing to have his more pressing work over and done with, at least for the time being.

For months there had been rumour and counter-rumour concerning the Royalist and Parliamentary factions recruiting and drumming up support. Preston and the Fylde were largely in favour of the King, although even here, there were many who wished Parliament to gain the ascendancy. There were stores of munitions at Lancaster and Liverpool, which Lord Strange, son of the old Earl of Derby, who was Lord Lieutenant of the Shire, had taken into his own keeping in July.

He did this to prevent them falling into Parliamentary hands. Manchester, a primarily pro-Parliamentary town, also had a store of munitions, which Lord Strange had stored in his own house there. Unfortunately for him, word got out to his opponents so they broke into his house and transferred the weapons somewhere else. At first he had admitted defeat, but in this month of September he had determined to try again. He found a thousand pikemen barring his way, so he camped outside the town and tried to negotiate for some of the weapons. His force, though considerable was not enough for a proper siege. Time went by, but the town refused to surrender. He asked for £1,000 in compensation, then for just 200 muskets, each time being stoutly refused, until in the end, the Mancunians replied that they would not give him, "so much as a rusty dagger." He had to withdraw, finally admitting defeat, and Manchester had irrevocably declared in favour of the Parliament.

Richard heard this from various sources and it appeared that matters were coming to a head at last. Royalist recruiting forces led by Sir Gilbert Hoghton, Lord Strange's Deputy, and Sir Thomas Tyldesley, from Gawthorpe Hall, near Burnley, had passed among the neighbouring villages, and taken many men, sometimes by force. Adam Morte, of Preston, who was married to Sir Thomas Tyldesley's daughter, (his second wife) Alderman of the Council, and about the only Royalist one, was away at this moment gathering troops in the King's name. He had been appointed a Commissioner of Array for this purpose.

On the Parliament side, Richard Shuttleworth, M.P. for Preston, now a Colonel, and Alexander Rigby, M.P. for Wigan, were doing the same, as was Ralph Assheton of Middleton.

So, Richard felt it was coming near the time when he must tear himself away from his wife and his home and declare himself for the Parliament's side.

This was why he was anxious to get the crop in as soon as possible. The trouble was, he didn't know how he was going to break the news to his wife, especially in her condition. But it must be done, and soon. Being Sir Gilbert's tenant (via Master Claythorne) it was a wonder he had not already been enlisted. Many of that worthy's tenants had been recruited already and had to leave their land and farms unattended.

This was what was worrying him most. He could not expect his father and brothers to help him as they were in like case and would have to leave their farm, if it became necessary. So, still feeling anxious and frustrated, he and his helpers laboured through the daylight hours, casting anxious glances at the sky, hoping that the fine weather would hold.

Jennet, and Mary also, whenever they could spare the time from their own tasks, came out to help, though Richard would not allow Jennet to do anything strenuous.

She laughed disdainfully, claiming that she was a strong and healthy female, and had worked hard all her life.

"But you were not about to have a child," he retorted.

"I should think not, when I was so young and not even wed yet," she flashed back.

But she knew how much he wanted this child and so she would do nothing to jeopardise its well-being, or even her own. So she contented herself with doing only the lightest tasks, and keeping them supplied with food and drink during those hot, tiring days. She knew, also, that he was worried about the impending clash of forces and why, though he had not discussed it with her as yet.

But, women's intuition made her privy to the workings of her man's mind and she wished she could do something to ease it.

After the harvesting was done and the grain sent to the miller to be ground, Richard began to make his preparations. He had a musket and breast-plate, part of the weaponry the King had ordered every man to have, only a few years before when he was fighting against the Scots. Many local, older men had seen service in these battles, and some had even seen service in France, which made them all the more reluctant to take part in any more fighting.

Richard brought out his meagre armour and the rusty musket one evening, and began to clean them and oil them. Jennet paled when she saw what he was doing. She dropped her sewing on to the table and pressed her hands to her mouth.

"Oh, my husband, has it finally come to it?" she cried, "you are leaving to fight for the Parliament?"

"Yes, I must it seems. William told me today, he means to go before the week is out."

"But he has only been wed but a few short weeks. How can he leave poor Alice so soon?"

"How can I leave you, my love, when we have been wed only a few short months, and you with child? Alice, at least, has not conceived, as far as I know. And there is nothing else we can do. The Royalist Officers have been in Broughton and taken away five men and a boy of fifteen to be trained in their service. Henry is mad to go, too, but my father will not let him. He is not sixteen until February, but the swears he will go then. My father will not go, he says someone must stay to care for our two farms and households, but I fear the soldiers will not worry overmuch about that, when he is a hale man and not yet fifty."

It was Wednesday and two brothers were to leave on Saturday in the morning. Amidst all their frantic preparations, Jennet had not had time to think. But at supper on Friday, she stopped suddenly, dropping her spoon on to the table. There was but this one evening left, and the night, before dear Richard would be gone! Her heart sank in awful fear. Suppose . . . suppose. . . . But she thrust the thought away, suppressing her dread with an effort that left her feeling sick and weak. She would not let him see the grief and fear that was in her, for she would not add to his already burdened heart.

So she kept up a cheerful chatter, covering up her accident with the spoon with a jest about her clumsiness. But Richard was not fooled; he had seen the look on her face and knew what she was thinking, with the perceptiveness of love.

"Dear courageous little wife of mine," he thought, "God grant that she will come through this safely, and with no more sorrow than she has already had to bear."

The rest of the evening passed and then it was bed-time. They were all retiring early, because of Richard's early start. Jennet acted with a forced gaiety, fighting to hold back the tears that kept threatening to spill over. The others were all in a subdued mood; no one had spoken much that evening. Even Jess's usually surly expression had changed to one of concern.

Richard gave them their last minute instructions, bade them all to remember them well, asked them to take care of their mistress and themselves, for on the morrow he would not have time to spare in lingering farewells, and thanked them for their help in the past. It was almost, thought Jennet, like a dying man taking farewell of his family and friends, but no - she must not think such gloomy thoughts. She mustn't . . . she mustn't. . . !

They were long in getting to sleep that night, despite their good intentions to get a good night's rest before their early rising tomorrow.

They lay in each other's arms, Jennet and Richard, each thinking their own thoughts, until finally sleep overcame their weary minds and bodies.

They were all up betimes next morning, long before dawn, and were eating a hasty breakfast when they heard the clip-clop of horses' hooves coming into the farmyard. It was brother William, accoutred and armed, leading another horse, already saddled for Richard. He was taller than Richard and more burly about the shoulders, but with the same unruly shock of hair and brown eyes that looked steadfastly into the eyes of whomever he was speaking to. His face was set and stern this morning, but he gave a courteous greeting to them all, before bidding his younger brother to hasten for they must be off before the light began to appear in the dawn skies.

Richard hurriedly fastened his knapsack to the saddle and hoisted the strap of his musket over his shoulder. Then he shook the hands of Jess, Jack and Mary (the last two were quietly weeping) before turning to his wife. She threw her arms about his neck, and he held her close as though he would never let her go. They kissed, and he whispered, "God have you in his keeping, my darling," then he tore himself away and was in the saddle with a leap!

Jennet prayed too. "And God keep you safe and bring you back to me," when with a final wave, they turned the horses round and went out of the gate and across the fields at a gallop. She stood there for a long moments, hands tightly clasped, murmuring over and over again, "Oh, Richard, will I ever see you again? Richard, Richard, my only love! You must come back, you must come back!"

Mary took her back into the kitchen and sat her down by the fire trying to calm her distress, but without much success for she was half distraught herself. Jack still wept in the corner, knuckling his eyes and sniffling. Then, suddenly, old Jess startled them all.

"Come on!" he almost shouted, taking Jack by the collar, "come ye lazy, womanish, bawling lout. There's work to be done. Yon cows will not wait for their milking while ye sit and weep like a maid."

He jerked the hapless lad to his feet and marched him to the door, and Jack, shocked out of his wits, stopped crying, and went meekly enough, wiping his eyes on his sleeve.

Jennet and Mary too were startled by this totally uncharacteristic behaviour of Jess's, and began to pull themselves together with an effort.

"Yes, it is true," said Jennet sadly, as she and Mary began to clear away the remains of their breakfast and to start their daily tasks, "it is true enough. Though all your world may lie shattered about you, life must go on."

CHAPTER SIX

Over a month passed before there was any news of Richard or William. Jennet received a brief letter, evidently written in haste, in which Richard said they had made contact with Colonel Shuttleworth's force after days of riding hither and thither, searching for the Parliamentary Army. Thy had had to hide on numerous occasions while the Royalists went by and once had narrowly escaped being discovered when some King's men had stayed for the night in a barn in which they were hidden in the straw.

Richard was well and in good spirits, except that he missed her sorely and hoped that things were well with her and the farm. He did not say where they were, but added that they were preparing to march on a venture of importance. He said also that Colonel Shuttleworth had received William and him in a very cordial manner and they, being in possession of horses, had been incorporated into the cavalry.

When she read out this last to the assembled household that evening, Jack let out a whoop and threw his hat in the air. "Hurrah for M'maister Richard," he yelled, capering about the room. "H'he be a g'good 'un. W'wish I w'were theer t'to see un!"

The lad had swiftly recovered from his initial resentment against Richard, as someone who was taking his beloved mistress's affections away from him, as he had thought and as time went on and she showed no lessening of her kindness and fondness, Jack was won over and indeed, had developed a sort of hero-worship of his master.

Mary had listened with shining eyes and clapped her hands with delight. "Ee, Mistress, it be reet good news. Wait till ah tell mi' muther. "Er'll be that pleased, but wheer can they be a'gooing?"

Jennet wondered too. It was not until some time later that she heard what the 'venture of importance' was.

It seems that Sir Gilbert Hoghton, the ardent Royalist, knowing that further munitions were urgently needed by their forces and hearing of Lord Strange's (now the Earl of Derby on the recent death of his father) abortive attempt to gain those in Manchester, had decided to take those which were stored at Whalley. He and his small force had accordingly done this and proceeded to Blackburn, where on the 27th October they had bedded down for the night, feeling that they had made the town a Royalist stronghold.

By that same evening, Colonel Shuttleworth had got wind of this and called a meeting on Enfield Moor to the north of the town.

It was decided to attack, for they knew that those munitions were of the utmost importance to their cause. As they drew near, the guards posted on the Parish Church spotted them and opened fire. The Parliament men, who had divided into two companies, attacked on two sides and after two hours of fierce fighting broke through.

Sir Gilbert fled, leaving many of his men prisoners. Colonel Shuttleworth addressed those taken prisoner who were brought before him, and bade them be honest men and go home and stay there and so they were released.

Richard and William were in the attacking force and had nothing but praise for Colonel Shuttleworth's justice and mercy to the prisoners, most of whom were the 'clubmen whom Sir Gilbert had recruited. These were bands of poorly trained men armed with anything they could pick up, clubs, pitch-forks, staves, in fact anything at all. They were not in this conflict because they were in favour of one side or the other, but for the hope of plunder.

William had been slightly wounded in the arm, which did not greatly inconvenience him and Richard, to his own amazement had escaped unscathed. It had been in some trepidation that he had advanced with the small force towards Blackburn, after having only two weeks training. So, feeling completely untried and unsure of himself, he went forward. In the heat of battle there had been no time or opportunity to feel fear. Afterward, there had been the reaction, when he had leaned against the nearest wall, trembling and feeling sick. William, when they spoke together, had confessed to feeling the same, so Richard didn't feel so ashamed. They were both elated however, when their commander commended them for their behaviour during the action, and promoted them to corporals.

Richard communicated all this to his wife as soon as he was able, in a long letter which took him many hours to write. He, with his brother, were now garrisoned at Blackburn and were there when Sir Gilbert made another abortive attempt to storm the town on Christmas Eve.

The baronet gave up on Christmas evening, having got no nearer than a quarter of a mile from the town. His soldiers and clubmen were glad to go home to eat their Christmas fare in peace, albeit a little belatedly. They had had enough of sitting there in the freezing cold and at Christmas-tide too! There were no casualties, except the poor farmer, on whose land they were encamped. They had taken his barn-doors, with carts, wheels, and other equipment to burn for their fires and had eaten his store of meal and beef and other foodstuffs, and with no recompense, either. The only other damage done was by a ball from the Royalist's field-piece, which had penetrated into a house in Blackburn and pierced a huge hole in the bottom of a frying pan, or so it was reported by the jubilant Parliamentarians.

At Gregson's Farm, which was still so called despite its change of tenant, Jennet spent a miserable Christmas. She knew where Richard was garrisoned from his letter and that he hated writing, for it was still so difficult for him, so it was even more precious for that reason.

How she wished he had been allowed to come home for a few days, a few hours even. But she was not then to know of the events which were taking place at Blackburn.

Will Towneley had invited her to spend Christmas with them. She could bring Jess and Jack, too, he said, knowing she would not leave them to fend for themselves at Christmas. Mary had gone home for a couple of days, armed with whatever good cheer Jennet could spare.

Will had urged her, feeling concern for his daughter-in-law, poor lass, with no husband at hand to aid and comfort her, and she now in her seventh month. True, he now had another daughter-in-law who was bereft of her husband, young Alice, but she was not pregnant and she lived with Will and Granny and young Henry and did not want for friends. Granny's health had not been good these past months, worrying herself sick over her two grandsons she was, and starting to show her great age, so it was well that she had Alice to help her. Not that *she* was much help, he felt sadly.

Despite Will's urgings, however, Jennet would not leave the farm, even for a few hours. There was always the chance that Richard would get the opportunity to spend a short time at home and she must be there to greet him if he should come unexpectedly. It would be a shame if he should arrive expecting her to be there and find no loving welcome, even though she would be only a very short distance away, at his father's house.

So she was adamant, but thanked him warmly for his offer and his concern.

"Do not concern yourself, Sir," she assured him, "I am in good health and do not want for anything. I would not want to be away from home in case my husband should chance to come back. But I thank you most heartily and shall not forget your constant care and kindness to me."

So, Will had to leave it at that, but promised to call as often as he was able, as indeed he had been doing since his two sons had departed to see that she was in good health and did not need anything. Alice and Henry had also visited her, Henry full of the plans he had to fight for the Parliament as soon as he could get away. Alice was a pretty young thing, Jennet thought, though a bit flighty. She had fair, curling hair and large, blue eyes and rosy dimpled cheeks. Jennet could tell she resented Granny's iron rule of the Towneley household and of Alice herself, feeling that as wife to Will's eldest son she should be mistress. But Granny wasn't about to hand over to some sixteen-year-old chit of a lass.

"But," remarked Alice, a little spitefully, "she cannot last for ever. She must be well over seventy and has been ailing these two months past. It won't be long now, you just wait and see. . . ."

She was careful not to say any of this in Henry's hearing when he accompanied her, for she knew he loved old Granny. He was her darling, the youngest of her grandsons, although she loved them all.

Jennet had planned that this should be a wonderful Christmas, before the possibility of civil war had become a reality, for it would be Richard's and her's first Christmas together. Christmases with her father had been austere affairs. True to his strict Puritanism, he had frowned upon merry-making or any kind of jollity.

She had been surprised to find that the Towneleys, though they were Presbyterians and hated Popery, were much more moderate in their outlook. Richard loved to laugh and share a joke, as she well knew.

She remembered the silly play-acting he had indulged in, the day she had broken the news of their coming child. Looking down, she put a hand on her swollen stomach, feeling the child move within her. It seemed very active, always kicking. Mistress Thomson told her that was a sign it would be a boy.

She hoped so, for Richard's sake, and her own, for she would love a small replica of her darling husband. She had already decided on the name 'Richard John', for her husband and her father. She had not even thought of a girl's name, so sure was she that it was a male child she was carrying.

So Christmas came and went and Richard did not come. By the first week in January in which was her birthday, she was becoming desperate for news.

Will Towneley came over, with a letter from William, in which he said that Richard had been sent to Manchester where Sir John Seaton had arrived with a company of dragoons, not long after Lord Derby's attempt on that stoutly Parliamentarian town. He also spoke of Sir Gilbert Hoghton's attempt to regain control of Blackburn at Christmas and how it had misfired.

Will also told her of the surprising news that Adam Morte, an Alderman of Preston Council, had been elected Mayor at the Mayoral elections in October, but had refused to take up the position.

"In fact," said Will, "he was not even in the district, being away recruiting for the King. So, the council fined him, in his absence, the sum of 100 marks for his contumacy, which if not paid within a certain time, would be taken from his goods and chattels. I cannot understand why they chose him in the first place, for the Council, to my certain knowledge, are all for the Parliament, while he is an ardent Royalist. It may be that they wished to be able to watch him and have him in a position where they could do so." He scratched his head in perplexity, then continued, "At any rate, I hear that he is back in the town, and whether he has decided to take up the office of Mayor, which Master Werden has had to carry on with, I do not know, but I believe that he is supervising the fortifying of the three bars of Fishergate, Friargate and Churchgate."

Jennet was not really interested in Will's account of the contumacy of Master Adam Morte. She was wishing there had been more news of Richard.

"You are sure, father-in-law, that William has written nothing more about Richard? Why was he sent to Manchester? It is strange that he did not write me a brief note to tell me before he went."

"Soldiers are not always privy to the workings of their commanders' minds, lass and perhaps he had not time to do so. Sometimes they have to be ready to go at a moment's notice. But do not worry about it and trust in God."

But she could not help worrying about it, as Will well knew, though he tried to comfort her. "I think you should consider coming to Whitegate Farm until after the birthing of your child," he urged. "My mother is ailing, it is true, but you would have Alice with you and you are of an age. I had been thinking of sending her over here to stay with you, but with my mother being so ill, she is needed there."

Not that she is of much use, he thought, she thinks more of how she looks and is forever preening herself instead of getting on with her household chores.

Jennet politely refused, declaring that she was perfectly alright and that Mary was a good help to her, and in any case, it was but a short distance to Mistress Thomson's house, and Jack could reach her in a very short time when the time arose that she would be needed.

Will shook his head in frustration.

"You are very stubborn, lass, to be sure. Richard would not thank me if anything should go amiss with you or the child. But at least I have tried. It may be that you will be glad to come to us when your time draws nigh, I confess I do not like to think of you here alone, with only a young maid, an old man and a simpleton to take care of you."

Jennet started to protest that Jack was not a 'simpleton', but thought better of it. What was the use? Her father-in-law like the rest of their neighbours had preconceived ideas about Jack's mental capabilities - or lack of them.

After Will had left, trudging away towards his own farm, through the fine layer of crunchy snow which had fallen overnight, she looked at the bulky package Will had thrust upon her on departing. "In honour of your birthday," he had said. "And for the baby, from Granny."

Tomorrow, the 5th, was her birthday. She was now eighteen and by her standards, well advanced in years, but she was not too old nor too saddened and worried by Richard's continued absence not to feel excited and thrilled at the unexpected gift. She had not been used to receiving presents upon her natal day, nor any other time, until Richard's advent.

So, with trembling fingers she drew off the covering of clean, white linen. 'Tis will do for the making of a baby's gown, she thought, as she put it aside. Inside she found a beautiful, crocheted shawl, soft and warm to the touch. Granny must have spent many hours making this with her painfully arthritic hands, she mused.

How very kind and thoughtful of the poor old lady. She was now so ill, too.

"I must go and pay her a visit," she resolved." And take something for her."

She turned to the other item which had fallen on the table when she lifted the shawl, and gasped in delight.

She lifted the folds of dark blue silk, lined with coney, and draped it about herself. A cloak! And such a cloak, edged with ruched maroon velvet and with a capacious hood. Quickly, she lifted down the large, shallow copper pan, and propped it up against the back of the settle beside the fireplace. She was turning this way and that, luxuriating in the feel of the fur against her neck and arms, when Mary came in from her work in the dairy.

"Why, Mistress!" she gasped. "I thowt it were a fine lady come to visit thee, an' 'tis thi'sel looking lak a princess, to be sure. But wheer hasta getten such finery?"

Jennet told her and then Mary had to exclaim over the soft, intricately worked shawl.

" 'Tis a marvel, indeed, Ma'am. Yon old dame allus were a great un wi' her fingers. Mi' muther's oft towd me about it. 'Tis a pity she be so ill, and her hands full o' t'rheumatics. And that cloak, why it must a' cost a mint o' money!"

Jennet, still preening herself in front of the makeshift mirror and Mary, her voiced raised in admiration of the gifts, did not hear the crunch of snow outside in the farmyard, nor the quiet opening of the kitchen door. If they had, they would probably have thought it only Jess or Jack, or even Harry, who were busy in the barn mending the farm implements, their usual winter occupation, apart from tending the cattle.

It was Richard who stood there quietly watching them, his clothes travel-stained and dusty, and dropping with weariness. He stood with his hand on the latch, with the late afternoon sun behind him, turning the snow to pink where it struck the corner of the yard.

"Mary, did you not close the door properly when you came in?

There is a draught." Jennet, still admiring herself, did not turn round until, faintly reflected in the shiny surface of the pan, she saw a tall figure which was not Mary's by any stretch of the imagination, loom up behind her. She whirled round, knowing at once who it was.

"Richard, oh Richard!" She threw her arms around his neck and he drew her close. They stood, locked in each other's arms, oblivious to all.

Mary, after one frenzied shriek of "Master Richard!" had stood with her hands to her face, for a second, then rushed out to the barn, to tell the others that their master was home.

However, their joy was short-lived, for as Richard explained, "I can only stay for two hours at the most. I was sent to Manchester with urgent dispatches for Sir John Seaton, the usual messengers being already sent on errands to other Commanders and now, Sir John has entrusted me with his reply to Colonel Shuttleworth, to whom I must repair as soon as maybe. But Sir John, when I told him how much I would like to see my dear wife whose birthday is tomorrow, gave me leave to break my journey to here provided I made good time from Manchester to Preston. And I did! I think I almost killed the poor horse, so fast did I urge him. I am glad you Jess and Jack, have tended him and given him food, and he has had a chance to rest a while, for he is a willing beast."

"And his Master was in like case," remarked his wife. "I thought you were like to faint from tiredness. 'Tis a pity you must go on tonight, for you are in need of a good night's rest."

"T'will not take long from here to Blackburn and I am much refreshed from this rest and the food you have set before me."

They were seated on the settle before the fire, Richard with his arm about his wife and she holding his hand. Then he, remembering the scene as he entered the kitchen, asked where she had got her finery. She told him and took up the shawl, his grandmother's gift, to show him.

The others, after they had crowded in to see him and offer their greetings and hear his news, had tactfully withdrawn to the barn to allow husband and wife their short time together. He asked how his family had fared and she told him all was well but for his grandmother who was not in good health.

"What, Granny ailing?" he cried incredulously. "It is impossible! She has always been so hale. I used to think she would go on forever. She has never changed since I was a child. But - she is a great age, after all, and I fear she has not got over William's and my departure," he finished soberly.

Jennet tried to cheer him, "It may be just a slight unease of the joints she suffers from. You know how stiff she gets in her hands and lower limbs, like Jess does."

"I wish I could spare the time to go over and see them all, but 'tis impossible. You must tell them how I had to make haste to get back and give my loving greetings. But how are you, my sweet wife? I see the little one grows apace." He patted her swollen belly and was amazed and delighted to feel the movement of the child.

"You don't think I look gross and ugly?" enquired Jennet anxiously.

"You are more beautiful than ever. When I walked in and saw you parading in your silken cloak, I thought you looked like a vision of loveliness. But even in your black gown and with your cap all awry and your belly as big as a house you look like a queen." They both laughed at the reference to his joke made many months ago.

Suddenly remembering, he put his hand inside his jerkin and pulled out a small packet.

"I almost forgot. Here, for your birthday."

She opened it to find a small chased silver locket on a slender chain, and exclaimed in rapture.

"Oh, Richard 'tis exquisite. I am becoming quite a fine lady with all these wondrous gifts. But wait, one more thing is needed."

She rose, and before he could protest, seized her scissors and snipped a small lock of his fair hair. Opening the locket she placed it inside.

"Now, you may put it on. I will wear this always and keep a

part of you always with me." He put the locket round her neck and fastened the tiny clasp, kissing her neck as he did so.

"I think, sweet Jennet, that it is only fair that we exchange tokens."

He took the scissors and cut a tiny curl from the nape of her neck where her brown hair clustered in damp tendrils from the heat of the fire. She wrapped it in a scrap of cloth and tied it with a thread and gave it to him. He set it securely in the inside pocket of his jerkin on the left side and patting the spot said, "I will keep it here next to my heart, as a talisman and a token of our love."

Jennet clasped the locket tenderly, "And I too, Richard," she whispered fervently.

Then catching sight of the old, wooden-cased clock on the dresser, he rose regretfully. "Sweetheart, I must go." Going to the door he shouted to Jack to fetch his horse from the barn.

Then he took Jennet in his arms and kissed her, holding her so tightly that she almost cried out in pain, but would not, because it was pain she would endure gladly.

He whispered, "Take care of yourself and our son. I do not know when we shall meet again. I pray God it may be soon. Farewell, my dear love."

He tore himself away, said a brief farewell to Mary and Jess, huddling in the doorway of the barn, and to Jack who was holding his horse, mounted, and with a last long look at his wife, waved his hand and was gone.

Jennet turned sadly back into the house, joined by the others. Mary and Jack talked all evening of their master's brief visit. Jess sat silent, puffing at his old clay pipe and glancing every now and then at Jennet, sitting huddled by the fire, clutching the locket in white-knuckled fingers and staring, blind eyed, into the embers. He was not without perception, old Jess.

She was filled with vague forebodings which beset her all the evening, and when at last she slept that night, encroached upon her dreams, turning them into nightmares.

CHAPTER SEVEN

By the beginning of February, they had most of the ploughing finished, for the winter had not been as harsh as last year. There was much rain, however, which made ploughing difficult, turning the fields into quagmires. Harry and Jack laboured manfully, returning from the field each day, covered to the thighs with mud and dropping with exhaustion.

Jess helped them as much as he could, whenever his rheumatism would allow.

Harry was a stocky, cheerful young man, always ready to make a suggestion that would help with the running of the farm, He advised Jennet to get some casual labour, to help to get the ploughing finished sooner.

He knew of several men, most of them older types who would be glad of a day or two of labour. They were those who had escaped the muster of men by the recruiting forces of either side. Harry himself had only evaded the Royalist impressment of the men of Broughton village, because he had been working at Gregson's farm at the time.

So Jennet gave her assent to him hiring a man to help, though gazing ruefully at her dwindling funds, she realised that she would have to be very careful in future. She liked Harry and his bluff, hearty manner. There was no nonsense about him and she congratulated herself on her astuteness in persuading her husband to hire him.

But she noticed he was getting restive of late and wondered what could be the matter. It was Mary who told her, having wormed it out of Jack who had been reluctant to speak of what had been told to him in confidence.

Harry, it seemed, was planning to join the Parliamentary army, but had hesitated to leave his mistress without a substitute for himself. Hence his suggestion that they should hire someone to help with the ploughing, whom she could take on permanently if necessary.

When she asked him about it, he flushed painfully, but admitted it, begging her pardon if he seemed disloyal but she must see that a young man like himself could not remain safely working on the farm when his master and others like him were away fighting for the Parliament.

"What do your mother and sister say?" asked Jennet. "And Alison, have you told her?"

"Aye, and she thinks 'tis mi' bounden duty to go," he replied. "Mi' muther an' our Sal wain't be so keen when Ah tells 'em, but they'll 'ave ta wear it."

So she had to let him go and could not blame him. He was only doing what hundreds of others were doing at this moment, joining up to fight for what they thought was right, be it for King or Parliament.

The new man, who brought his young son with him, was a good enough worker, although not as good as Harry. He begged Jennet to let his boy and him stay. They would stay in the barn and work for their keep.

He was from a village near Blackburn, his wife had died of the plague some years before, along with his two daughters. He had only the boy who, almost twelve, looked younger, thought Jennet, gazing at his thin, pale face and small, bony body.

"We have no home," went on the man, a pinched, grizzled man in his forties, whose name, he said, was Sam Grisby. "The Royalists burned our cottage when they marched on Blackburn, and took all our food and livestock. We fled, while they were slaughtering the pigs and made our way as best we could to my sister's at Broughton. But she has a large family and her husband has been taken for a soldier. So they have little enough for themselves, indeed are nearly starving. We were glad enough when Harry Baines said we could come here to find work. So please, Mistress, of your charity, say we may stay." He looked pleadingly at her, clasping his hands in supplication.

Jennet, her eyes on the child and his puny little body, agreed they could stay and work on the farm.

"But only for your food and lodging, mind," she admonished. "My resources are limited and will not stretch to another wage." There was Harry's wage, of course, which would not now be paid, but she had resolved to hoard as much as possible and anyway, there would be two more mouths to feed and the boy looked as though he needed feeding up for a few months before he would be much use to them.

"Thankee, Mistress," said Sam, going down on his knees to kiss the hem of her gown, "Jamie and me be that grateful. He be a strong lad, despite his looks and we will work till we drop for thee." He rose, nudging the lad, who had been gazing entranced at Jennet, and at the neat kitchen.

Urged by his father, he stammered his thanks and sketched a clumsy bow.

Jennet gave them food, which they devoured ravenously, then sent them off to the barn to find Jack who was cleaning the ploughshare, before starting on the few remaining areas of ground to be ploughed.

Jack seemed to have grown up a lot in the past few moths. Now fifteen, he was growing tall and filling out in an alarming manner, which taxed all Jennet's and Mary's ingenuity to keep him warmly and adequately clothed.

He didn't really care for Sam, who tended to boss him because of his age, but the boy, Jamie, he took under his wing and made much of, finding someone at last who was smaller and weaker than himself.

Jennet had determined to keep the farm going as Richard would have wished, but now, only weeks from her confinement, she was feeling low and dispirited, hardly able to cope with the constant demands made on her. Fortunately, Jack had learnt enough about the working of the farm to know what was required to be done. But there were always decisions to be made, which the others always left to her. Feeling totally inadequate at times, she often crept into her bed at night and sobbed herself to sleep, feeling Richard's absence acutely.

Mary helped, of course, in every way she could. She was worried about her mistress, watching the weary way she dragged herself about. She was sure Mistress Towneley was harming herself and the baby by the way she insisted on seeing to everything herself and working so hard. But it was no use protesting, mistress wouldn't listen.

Before Richard had left, he had started excavating, with Jack's and Harry's help, a fair-sized cellar under the barn, shoring it up with beams and tree-trunks. They had finished it as soon as they could after he had gone and transferred most of their stores and some equipment. The reason for this being Master Towneley's advice to his son to find somewhere to hide his supplies of food, both for themselves and the farm animals and other essentials, for having seen service himself, years ago in France, Will knew the ways of soldiers on the march.

It was disguised under a cunning layer of earth and straw and had steps leading down to it... It could be used as a hiding-place, if necessary, for several days, or weeks at a pinch. Jennet had ordered a large container of water and other necessities taken down. When she first surveyed the cellar after it was completed, she had thought what a good idea it was, for down there in the cool darkness, food would keep so much longer, even were there no emergency.

Will Towneley came over the next day, which was the 5th February, a Sunday, the day after Henry's birthday, when he became sixteen. Will was greatly disturbed, for that morning he had found Henry's bed had not been slept in, and the pony had gone from the stable.

"He has gone, Jennet, as he said he would. But just lately he had not spoken of it, so I thought he had given up the idea. Fool that I was! I should have watched him more closely. Now all my sons have gone!"

"But, Father-in-law, you could not know. And Henry is of an age to join the army. Many have had to go who were not even his age. Do not, I pray you, distress yourself. If he should manage to join up with William's and Richard's company, they will take care of him and try to see he comes to no harm."

"Not only that is troubling me, my daughter. My mother is gravely ill and I think, will die. I did not want to tell her of this news, knowing how she dotes on the lad, though t'would be hard to keep his absence from her, seeing he would sit with her for much of his free time each day. But that foolish lass, Alice, had to acquaint her with it, out of spite. I swear she shrieked when she was told and swooned away, from which she cannot be awakened. The apothecary has been but he can do nothing."

Jennet exclaimed, and raised her hands in sympathy with the poor man. He turned to go, saying he could leave Granny no longer, especially with that feckless daughter-in-law, Alice, looking after her. He thanked God he had at least one daughter-in-law with some sense about her.

But Jennet would not let him go alone. Calling to Mary, she gave the girl instructions to look after the men's welfare, and hastily putting some things into a basket, set out with Will back to Whitegate Farm.

It was difficult for her to walk the fairly short distance to Will's farm in her condition, over the marshy ground, but with Will assisting her, she managed it. He had protested, saying she should not be doing this, but she insisted and knowing of old his daughter-in-law's determined nature, he had to agree to her coming.

She found Granny, looking shrunken, and with a ghastly yellowish colour. She lay, dwarfed in the big four -poster, her body like a child's, hardly showing under the bulky counter-pane. She was breathing stertorously, and Jennet, with a pang remembered how her father had looked just so just before he died. It was obvious she had only a few hours to live.

She did what she could to make the old woman comfortable, bathing her face and hands and getting the little serving-maid to plump up the pillows. Granny never stirred, but seemed to sink further into unconsciousness as time went on.

Alice did nothing but crouch on a stool in the corner, sniffing and dabbing at her eyes, and peering slyly at Jennet, whenever she thought her sister-in-law could not see her.

Jennet hardly glanced at her, for she was engrossed in attending to Granny. Will came in, mutely appealing to Jennet but she shook her head sadly. He sat on the other side of the bed, holding his mother's hand and silently praying.

It was Jennet, of course, who noticed the change in the old lady; her breathing had become shallower until it could hardly be heard, and her face had assumed a peaceful expression. No more struggling for breath; no more worry over her family. Granny Towneley was dead.

Jennet rose, and pulled the counterpane over the now gently smiling face, and went round the bed to comfort the sobbing, grief-stricken Will.

Jack had come over as soon as he had the news from Mary that Jennet had gone over to Whitegate.

He was waiting in the kitchen of Will's house with his now ever-present companion, Jamie.

They helped her home, at least Jack did, Jamie was not big enough, but he carried the lantern to guide their footsteps. When they got home she sat down to write to Richard to inform him of Granny's death, and Henry's departure, and asked him to look out for the lad. She promised to do this for Will's sake, as well as her own; she knew he was too distraught to do so himself.

The next day, the 7th, dawned bright and clear, but with a strong wind blowing. During the morning, Jennet decided to go with Mary down to the cellar to check the supplies of food and grain. Their precious seed, saved from last year's crop was down there too. She wanted to know if it and the other supplies were keeping well. She remembered also, that they had not taken any candles down, so wanted to remedy that omission.

Mary followed her resignedly with the candles. She wanted to tell Jennet that with being so near her time, (it was only three weeks away according to the midwife's calculations) she should be taking things easy and not insist on doing things like this, but she knew what the result of that would be.

So down they went, Mary first lifting the carefully concealed trap-door, which was a cunning arrangement of boards plastered with mud and cow-dung, and with straw plentifully mixed with it. Then she assisted Jennet to climb down the steps. With the candle held high she inspected the underground room, carefully noted that no mildew was present on anything and the hams and bacon were in good condition. Mary deposited the spare candles in a safe place.

"Yes," said Jennet with satisfaction, "everything is in good order. It is dry and cool down here. It will be useful in summer to keep our more perishable goods."

They had started to ascend the steps up into the barn when they heard the sound of running footsteps coming into the barn. Jennet stopped with one foot on the lowest step and looked up through the square aperture of the open trap-door.

Sam Grisby appeared, his face flushed and agitated, dragging a protesting Jamie by the collar. He thrust the lad down the steps and came down himself, pulling the trap-door shut behind him. Jennet was dumbfounded.

"Sam, what is amiss?" Jennet made to go up to the steps again but the man pulled at her gown. "What are you doing?" she asked again.

"Hush, mistress, you must not make a sound. 'Tis the King's men. I'll swear 'tis those misbegotten Papists who burned my cottage and stole my food. They be a-coming here to do the same, and I'll not let them take me or my boy."

"But Jess and Jack are out there. We must warn them!"

" 'Tis too late, you would never reach them in time. The Royalists are even now coming across the fields and that's where the old man and the lad are."

"And you were with them!" cried Jennet. "Why did you not tell them to run to safety?"

"Aye." he said, shamefacedly. "But I were at the other end of the field, when I saw the cursed King's men coming. I can smell 'em a mile off. I shouted to Jess and Jack to run, but they didn't seem to hear. Then I grabbed Jamie and ran. I knew about this little hidey-hole since you sent me down t'other day to fetch a bag o' meal. I went to the house first to find you, I swear, but when I couldn't, I made for here. I'm thankful indeed you managed to get here yourselves. Now we must stay quiet and hope they will not find us for t'will be short shrift for us if they do."

Mary cried out in fear, but Sam put his hand over her mouth. "Be quiet, lass, if you value your life, or your honour." The boy crouched, sobbing quietly, until his father fetched him a clout across the ear, then he subsided, burying his head in his arms. Jennet and Mary clung together, hardly daring to breathe, leaning against a pile of sacks. There was a faint sound of manly feet in the farmyard. Sam blew out the candle and sat on the steps.

They could hear many confused sounds and then what sounded like shouted commands. Heavy footsteps came in to the barn and men's voices were heard. They seemed to be searching, dragging things about and poking everywhere.

Jennet, her heart pounding, prayed fervently they would not discover the trap-door. She wondered if Jess and Jack had got away.

"Oh, God, let them be safe!" she prayed, silently. The time dragged on, while the men overhead continued their search, cursing and swearing. Then at last they moved out of the barn. Confused noises were again heard from outside; it was difficult to tell what they were, but she was sure she could hear the cows lowing in a terrified manner. What was happening? She wanted to scream, to rush out and confront these devils, but she was held fast by her own fear and Mary's terrified grip.

Hours later, it seemed, though it was but ten minutes, she heard footsteps approaching the barn again. She stiffened with renewed terror, "Oh, pray they are not going to search again!" But it was just two voices she heard quite clearly. One, obviously an educated man, said, "You are sure, Fenton, the men searched in here thoroughly? The stores must be somewhere."

"Yes, Captain Standerby," the other voice replied, sounding like a person of humbler rank. "I was here myself, Sir, and found nothing. There was nothing in the house, either, and no sign of any womenfolk, except their clothes. Perhaps they were forewarned and went off with the stores beforehand."

"All right, Fenton, that will do. Tell Jackson to question the lad again. Though I doubt he will get much out of the idiot. The old man is past telling us anything, so we must make do with what we have."

And then they were gone, tramping out of the barn, but Jennet was not aware of it for she had fallen in a dead faint against Mary, who screamed in terror. But no one heard, up there, they were making too much noise themselves.

Just as they were beginning to think they were safe, Mary, holding the inert form of Jennet, and Sam and the boy, heard the crackle of flames and smelled the acrid odour of smoke.

Someone had fired the barn.

CHAPTER EIGHT

Jennet woke up later that same night, after the King's men had raided the farm. She looked about her dazedly. She was in bed in in her own room. It must be time to get up. Then why was Mary sitting by her bed? And who was that sitting on the other side? Oh, it was the midwife, Goodwife Thomson. But why was she here? Surely it was not time yet? She had said it would be another two or three weeks before her baby was due. Jennet tried to speak but the words would not come. Her throat felt raw and it ached. She wanted a drink of water.

The midwife rose and held a cup to her lips. Jennet drank the water gratefully.

"The baby...," she managed to whisper. It sounded like a croak. "Is it..?"

"The bairn is fine, mistress. Still in there and kicking mightily. Though how you have come through this without it being born before its time is a miracle. I always said you were a strong lass." She put down the cup and busied herself straightening the pillows and lifting Jennet to a more comfortable position.

Jennet tried to make sense of her words. Come through what? She turned to Mary, questioningly, but the girl could not meet her gaze and burst into tears. Mistress Thomson tut-tutted with annoyance. "A lot of good you are in a sick room," she chided, "you had better go and tell Master Towneley his daughter-in-law has come to herself."

Mary scuttled out of the room, trying vainly to stifle her sobs. Will came in, crossed to the bed and took her hand.

"Thank God you have come out of it," he said, "I thought you were going to die." She looked at him in puzzlement.

Die? What could he mean? Surely he must be talking about Granny? But she was dead. Jennet remembered being there in Will's house when the old woman had passed away.

Slowly, the events of the past twenty-four hours came back to her. She and Mary going down to the cellar and then Sam and Jamie rushing in. The terrible time they had spent listening to the Royalist soldiers poking and prying above them and the voices of the two men. She remembered one name clearly, Captain Standerby. And what was it they were saying? As realisation flooded over her she flung her arms out to Will, who caught her as she fell forward.

"Oh, God, no! What has happened to Jess and Jack? Are they alright? Tell me! For the love of God!"

"Hush, lass." He held her, soothing her, wondering how he was going to tell her. Well, she would have to know.

"Jack is alright. He was badly beaten by those fiends from hell when they tried to make him tell where the stores were. But he didn't tell. He was very brave."

"And - and Jess?"

Will paused for a moment, selecting his words, but there was only one way to say it. "Jess is dead, Lass," he said very gently. "But the Royalists didn't kill him. He went for them when they came into the field. One of them aimed a blow at his face, trying to stop him. He fell, but got up, and began to come at them again. Then he staggered and went down. It was his heart, so the apothecary says. It burst with the exertion and his anger. He was a good age, as you know. Jack saw it all, before they dragged him back to the house."

"Poor Jess," Jennet found herself saying, hardly taking it in. Later she would mourn the old man whom she had known nearly all her young life. "But Jack - I must see him. Is he badly hurt?"

"Not seriously, but he will be sore and a bit weak for a few days yet. He has been asking after you and is waiting anxiously in the kitchen."

"Can - can he come in?" Will looked at the midwife. She nodded reluctantly.

"For a few moments only. The apothecary said she must rest as much as possible."

When Jack came in, Jennet exclaimed in pity at his poor swollen face and the arm held up in a sling. He limped as he came slowly into the room, holding himself stiffly and wincing at the pain in his bruised ribs.

"Oh, my poor boy! you have suffered so much and been so brave. You saved us all and the stores, too. Master Towneley has told me how you defied those wicked men."

"T'were nothing much, Mistress," Jack muttered, standing beside her. "They th'thought I were an idiot, when I couldn't get the words out, so I acted so an' they g'gave up."

Jennet could not help but notice how Jack had almost conquered his stammer. There was a new dignity about him, despite the pain he must be suffering. It was as though the ordeal he had been through had finally, and painfully, dragged him over the threshold into manhood.

"Now you must rest and get better," she ordered, decisively, "there will be no work for you for a few days, my lad."

"Nor for you, mistress," broke in Mistress Thomson, shooing Jack out of the room. "It's peace and quiet for you, if you want to let that baby come to its full term."

Jennet lay for a while, thinking, trying to come to terms with the traumatic experience she had just come through. She patted the distended stomach under the bed-clothes and felt the strong movements of her unborn child.

At least, he seemed to be alright. He must be a strong child to withstand all this. Her thoughts turned to Richard. He must not hear of this. He would be out of his mind with worry. She knew he worried about her, as she did about him. What two people in love didn't ? She hoped everything was well with him, her dear husband.

They did not tell her right away of the full damage to the farm and the loss of the livestock.

For Jess, she grieved quietly. That poor old man. She pictured him trying to stop the Royalist soldiers; as well try to stop the rising of the sun. But he had tried, so bravely and so futilely and had died with the effort. For all his surliness and grumbling, she had been fond of him. He had been with them so many years. It would be strange, and painful too, not to see his hunched figure sitting in the corner near the fireplace, nor smell the smoke from his old pipe. She shed a tear for him and prayed that wherever he was now he would be walking straight and free, with no more aches and pains, and plenty of 'baccy' for his clay pipe. She was sure it would be so, despite the parson's sermons of hellfire and damnation for the wicked (which Jess was not) and a heaven with wings and harps and angels for the God-fearing.

She could not imagine Jess with wings and a harp. She fell asleep trying to picture it and smiled to herself.

Mistress Thomson, abetted by the apothecary, insisted on Jennet staying in bed at least two days. But on Wednesday she received an urgent message from the village that one of the cottager's wives had been brought to bed. So, making sure that Jennet was not in any danger of imminent childbirth herself and with many injunctions to her and to the others, she departed.

Jennet, feeling as well as she could be, stayed in bed for an hour after she had gone, then called Mary to help her to get up. Mary didn't want to; she feared what would happen when her mistress saw the damage and found out that so many of her precious things had been taken.

Jennet had wondered, of course, why the sheets and bed-covers had been changed. She knew they weren't hers. Mary had fobbed her off, saying the King's men had made such a mess of them, that they couldn't be used and Master Will had lent them his. It was partly true anyway. She had seen that Mistress Jennet's chest had been ransacked and the blue cloak had gone, when they had returned to the house after the Royalists had gone. Everything had been done to clean up the mess and with Will's assistance, to restore as much as possible. But it would not escape her mistress's notice, she knew.

But it had to be done, Jennet would not be gainsaid, as usual, and Mary hoped it would not prove too much of a shock to her.

She was surprised, therefore, when after she had helped her mistress to dress and assisted her into the kitchen, Jennet had stood for a long moment gazing round, had walked slowly over to the dresser, fingered one or two dishes and other kitchen utensils, stared at the fireplace and the long score marks on the oaken settle, and said slowly and quietly, "So they took everything, did they, and damaged what they could not?"

So it came out. Mary told her, stumbling over the words. "Aye, Mistress, they took pots and pans and smashed t'others. They took the linen and the curtains, and clothes and.."

"Clothes, did you say? Then my cloak is gone too" She paled, and put out her hand to the dresser to steady herself. Mary went to her, but was waved away as her mistress pulled herself together.

"That is not all, is it, Mary? There is more, isn't there? Now tell me everything, or I'll go and see for myself." She sat down at the table, which she could see had been hurriedly repaired and motioned the servant to sit beside her, "Come," she commanded, "tell me what they did and miss nothing out if you dare."

Mary, trembling, began to tell her of the events of Monday. She told how the Royalists had fired the barn and how Will had rescued them. How they had found that the livestock had been taken, leaving only old Betsy and a few chickens which had evaded capture. And how when they had entered the house they saw the senseless destruction and damage.

"I reckon they would have burned the house, too, but for it being stone-built, though the thatch and the furniture would have burned like tinder. But Jack said, for he were not senseless then, not till after did he pass out, that the men were called away because they'd spent enough time here and must be off."

Jennet clenched her hands. What would Richard say when he found out about this? He had built so many hopes on being his own master and making the farm pay.

All the animals gone, poor Darby and Dewdrop, the cow who had been her favourite. She consoled herself with the thought that they had saved most of the food and other essentials. At least, they would not starve, for a while, anyway. She resolved to confer with Will and ask his advice and help for he had promised to do all he could.

They must see what could be done about the barn. Maybe it could be repaired. She fingered the locket around her neck, with the lock of Richard's hair in it. For his sake, she vowed, she would carry on, and for the sake of his child.

At that moment in Blackburn, the Parliamentary army, with Richard, William and Henry amongst them, were preparing to march on Preston.

CHAPTER NINE

After the Royalists left Gregson's Farm, with the barn burning furiously, they clattered into Whitegates Farm, demanding food and supplies.

The officer, a Captain Roger Standerby, so he informed Will, required supplies of meal and oats and whatever else they could supply, as the farm they had just left did not seem to have any, or none that they could find. They were wanted at once as they had to leave immediately to take them to their headquarters where they were needed urgently. They had many wagons, Will noticed, and cattle tethered behind them. Probably taken, he thought, from some poor farmer.

He wondered which farm they had just left and guessed with a pang of apprehension that is must be Gregson's which was nearest.

Knowing that everything depended on his getting rid of these soldiers quickly, for he must get over to see how Jennet and her household had fared, he offered Captain Standerby whatever he had, which wasn't much, he said, as he was a poor man and his poor mother was even now lying dead upstairs, as the Captain could see if he chose. He offered the Captain a cup of ale, which was accepted gratefully. The supplies the men dragged out were meagre enough, a few sacks of grain and barrels of ale, but the officer took them without comment. He asked Will, however, where his sympathies lay.

"With the King, of course," replied Will, salving his conscience with the thought that it was imperative that he get rid of these marauding Royalists by whatever means. "My three sons are even now fighting in that cause." May the Lord forgive me! he prayed.

"Then you are to be commended." The Captain looked at him. "But you are not an old man and look well enough. Why, then, have you not enlisted?"

"It was my old mother, sir, she has been gravely ill and someone was needed to take care of her. But now, alas, she has died, and I intend after the funeral to do my duty." His grief was not forced, as the soldier could plainly see.

"I offer you my condolences then, and I am glad you are a loyal subject of His Majesty."

He saluted with a flourish of his feathered hat and ordered the troop to march out. They, grumbling and cursing, did so. Will waited impatiently, thinking what a rough lot they were, ill-disciplined and obviously disgruntled at their lack of plunder, and the rain which had started to fall.

As soon as he was sure they had gone he called for his man, Joseph, who with the others had run to hide as soon as they had seen the soldiers. It was raining hard now, and Will hurriedly put on his heavy jerkin and put a sack over his head and shoulders.

Joseph came out from his hiding-place, looking fearfully around.

"It's alright, man, they've gone. They didn't get much, Praise the Lord," Will said, thankful he had taken his own advice to Richard and hidden the bulk of his stores in a safe place.

They hastened over the now sodden fields towards his son's farm and with a sinking heart Will saw the smoke from the barn.

They found Jess lying across the furrows in the ploughed field. he was dead, but they could find no mark on him, save for a cut on his cheek. The plough stood halfway down a furrow with a patient Betsy still harnessed to it, the rain sloughing down her back and sides.

In the farm-yard, Jack lay badly beaten and unconscious, huddled in a corner. The cows were gone and the pigs and chickens, except for one or two of the latter who had escaped capture by flying out of their would-be captors' reach and were now disconsolately pecking around the puddles in the yard.

There was no one in the ransacked farmhouse, so Will turned to the smouldering barn. The downpour had put out the flames but the wooden structure was black and charred, and Will feared the roof might fall in. They returned outside and Will was about to turn away when he heard a faint cry. Could it be? Yes, it was, and he, followed more cautiously by Joe, rushed over to where he knew was the entrance to the underground store-room.

With hasty fingers he tore at the charred wood covering the trap-door. It was still hot, so he took the wet sacking from his shoulders and, wrapping it around his hands, cleared away the remaining debris. Joe, doing the same helped him.

His fingers trembling, he raised the trap-door and with a sigh of relief saw the figures huddled in the dim chamber.

Sam and Jamie, coughing, and half stifled, managed to get up the steps but Will and Joe had to carry the still unconscious Jennet and the half hysterical Mary, up and into the house.

Will took charge, and dispatched Joe to the village for Mistress Thomson and to the apothecary. Sam was able to help in fetching in poor Jack and tending to his wounds and the boy Jamie was sent to Whitegates Farm with instructions to Mistress Alice to send over some clean linen, for Jennet's bed had been stripped of everything, even the sheets.

Then they carried Jess's body home and unhitched poor patient Betsy from the plough. Will wondered why the King's men hadn't taken her, but judged the old plough-horse wasn't considered suitable for their requirements. Darby was taken, of course, as was all the other livestock. Poor Richard, thought his father, how will he take this? Jennet too. Richard would be lucky to come home to a wife and child, the way she is. I fear she may die, poor lass.

He looked at the darkening sky. Was it such a short time since he had gone over to see Jennet yesterday morning? So much had happened in those few short hours. Henry gone, his mother dead, and now this. He shook his head sadly. The Lord was sending him great tribulation, but he must pray for help and guidance to carry him through. If only William and Richard and young Henry were here to help him.

On Tuesday evening, the 7th, Sir John Seaton rode into Blackburn with a large force. They had marched all day through the rain, from Manchester, four or five companies joined at Bolton by a similar number. They had arrived wet through and exhausted, just as William and Richard had been amazed and delighted by the arrival of young Henry at their billet.

He had reached Blackburn on Sunday afternoon, on foot, for the pony had been stolen by a band of ranging clubmen while Henry had stopped to slake his thirst at a wayside tavern.

Arriving at the garrison, footsore and weary, he had been assigned to a company after offering his services and being enlisted.

It was not until Tuesday morning that he had been able to prevail upon his immediate officer to allow him to try and locate his brothers.

It had taken him nearly all day, but here he was, except that he must report back to his own company by nine o'clock, Lieutenant Harding would have him disciplined if he didn't and he did not want that after being an enlisted man for only a day and a half.

"I wish I could have joined your company, he went on. "But I was so relieved at finding the Parliamentary army and so tired after my journey that I contacted the first company I found after having trouble getting into the town in the first place. I think they thought I was a spy but I managed to convince them of my good intentions."

"How did you persuade Father to let you go?" asked William.

"I didn't," replied Henry. "I knew he would not agree, so I crept out early on Sunday morning and made off with the pony, but I didn't keep him long, worse luck!"

"You young scamp!" cried William. "But you should not have come away without his consent. He will be furious and it was unkind to leave him so."

Richard chipped in, for he was anxious to know how everyone was, especially his wife.

"They are all well," replied his brother, "except Granny, who as you know, has ailed for some months. But I do not think it is serious." They did not know, of course, of Granny's death, the letter Jennet had written was lying still unposted in the drawer of the kitchen dresser.

They talked for a while until it was time for Henry to rejoin his company, discussing the arrival of Sir John Seaton and his men and wondering what it portended.

By the following evening they knew. They were to march on Preston. All day it had rained but they set out on a clear evening, the rain having ceased. The troops from Manchester were still weary from their long march of the day before, but they were in good heart and moved with a will. They passed Hoghton Tower, still held by the Royalists and soon were going past Walton. Then there was the five-arched Ribble Bridge coming into sight. They crossed it before dawn and drew up in the fields to the south of the town.

Then they were given their orders. Part of the force, and Henry's company was among them, were detailed to go round to the west side of Preston and come at the Friargate Bars.

The town had been well fortified, if hurriedly, with earthen walls, faced with bricks and the Bars reinforced.

William and Richard found themselves near to the Churchgate Bars, to the east. They could see the defenders, who were ready for them, peering over the walls armed with pikes.

Adam Morte, the erstwhile Mayor, stood up and shouted his defiance.

Near to them an argument broke out between two companies as to who should break into the town first. The Captain of one of them resolved it by dashing forward with his sword held aloft, shouting, "Follow me, or give me up forever!" He scaled the wall, the men following and broke through the defences. Soon, the defenders had abandoned their pikes and they were fighting with swords. Richard found himself in the thick of it, with no knowledge of how he got there. He didn't know where William was.

Some yards further along the wall, Adam Morte's men were still thrusting at the attacking force with their pikes. They came at the Parliamentarians with a great shout and Richard found himself fighting desperately. Musket balls were flying all around.

They were firing from the Tower of the Parish Church. William was one of those who broke through the back of a house into

Churchgate and were immediately engaged by a Captain of Horse and his men. The Captain thrust at William but he evaded the sword and caught the man by his embroidered coat and dragged him to the ground where he quickly dispatched him. Seeing their Captain slain, the rest of the riders who were still able, scattered.

It took two hours to take the town. There were many dead and wounded among the defenders, corpses lying in the streets and in the houses. But there were only a few dead among the attacking force.

Among them was Richard, lying near the bodies of Adam Morte and his eighteen year old son, Seth.

William found Richard later, when the battle was over and he was searching for his brothers. Henry was slightly wounded in the leg and had conducted himself well for an untried boy. William had a sword thrust through his side but it was not serious. So after it had been hurriedly dressed he went looking for Richard.

And here he was, lying on the cold ground, a pike thrust piercing his body.

William knelt, weeping. He could not believe it. Richard and he had been close, closer even than most brothers. And now he was gone. How was he going to break this news to Jennet and to his father? Poor Jennet whose baby would never see its father. He got up after closing the open, staring eyes and covering the still face.

Some men who had been detailed to remove the bodies of the slain, paused by his side. They had a cart with them. One of them asked sympathetically, "Was he a friend of yours?"

William turned to them and asked them to be careful with the body, for he wanted to make arrangements for Richard to be sent home for burial.

"He was my brother, you see," he told them, simply.

Then he went off to break the news to Henry.

CHAPTER TEN

Sam and Jamie had taken to sleeping in the deserted shippon since their previous sleeping quarters had been destroyed. Sam marvelled why this, too, had not been burned, but reckoned that the 'clubmen' who had been with the Royalist party and who, he thought, had been responsible for most of the looting and damage, had not had time to do this last piece of wanton destruction when ordered away by their officer. The dairy, too, had largely escaped damage, except for churns of buttermilk overturned and butter-making equipment taken or broken beyond repair.

Jack was now sleeping on a made-up bed in the kitchen, at Jennet's insistence. She told him he must now consider himself one of the family, not that she or Richard had ever really treated him truly as a servant, but since his heroic behaviour in not giving away their hiding place, and so saving themselves and their supplies, she felt he deserved every privilege she could afford.

She was sure Richard would feel the same. Besides, Jack needed care still until his injuries were healed, although he insisted on attempting to do whatever he could. He often went out, slowly easing his way, to see what could be done and to keep an eye on Sam whom he didn't really trust. He hadn't forgotten how the man had made off from the field where they were ploughing, taking young Jamie, without a word of warning that the King's men were coming. Young Jamie was alright, he was only a child, so could not be blamed for his father's cowardice.

Jamie was only three or four years younger, but from his superior height and breadth and the few years older, Jack felt like an uncle towards the boy. Not that he, Jack, would like Sam Grisby for a brother. Jack didn't believe the story Sam told of going to the farmhouse first to warn Mistress Jennet either. He reckoned that the man had made directly for the store-cellar, his only thought being for his own, and his son's safety.

He had mentioned his distrust of Sam to Jennet but she had

brushed his suspicions away with a smile and told him to have more Christian charity and wouldn't anyone be afraid of the Royalists if they'd had his previous experience of them?

He was not to be convinced, however, and continued to keep his eye on Sam.

Just after dawn on a cold, clear morning, in the shippon where he lay with his father, Jamie woke up. He lifted his head to see if it was morning but there was hardly any light coming through the chinks in the walls and from round the door. The window was covered by a thick piece of sacking, so no light came in there. It must be very early, too early to get up. They didn't have to get up betimes, these days, with no milking to be done. So why had he wakened up so soon? He usually lay asleep, dead to the world, until his father shook him roughly and bade him bestir himself.

It was cold, too, his nose felt icy. He burrowed further into the straw, pulling the sacking over his head and snuggling closer to his father's sleeping body.

Then he heard it again. It sounded like a dull boom. He sat up, drawing the sacking round him and listened hard. Faintly he heard the sound of shots, then after a long interval the low boom. What could it be?

Gingerly, he eased himself away from his father's side. He'd catch it from Pa if he disturbed him before it was time.

Stepping carefully, he tip-toed to the door, opened it quietly and slipped outside closing it behind him. He shivered in the cold air and there was a slight wind blowing.

Then he heard the sounds again, more clearly this time. Glancing at the kitchen window, he could see a faint light inside. Someone was up. He'd go across and ask whoever it was about the noise, and maybe they'd know. He'd be warmer there, too, if the fire had been re-kindled, and perhaps there'd be a bite to eat. He was starving, but then he always was. He was glad he and Pa had come here, at least you got a decent meal every day, sometimes even two or three. It was like heaven after the way they'd lived before.

He opened the kitchen door and poked his head through. Oh, it was Master Jack. He was glad, he liked him. Master Jack was trying to blow up the fire, without much success, what with having his arm tied up. Jamie ran over and offered to help. Jack relinquished the bellows thankfully and straightened up, wincing.

"What be you a-doing up s-so early?" he enquired. "C-couldn't you s-sleep?"

"I was wakened by them noises," answered the boy, blowing the bellows vigorously. He was feeling warmer already, as the fire began to perk up. Jack carefully laid another turf on top with his good arm.

"W-what noises?"

"Sounds lak shootin' or sumthin'. Comin' fra Preston way, Ah thinks. An' they's a boomin' sound, too."

Jack looked at him questioningly, but he didn't say anything. Then he went to the door, opened it and stood listening. The boy was right, there was a faint sound of firing and occasionally a louder sound like a short peal of thunder. It must be coming from Preston, though he had no way of knowing for sure. Sounds carried far on clear mornings like this and the wind was coming from the south east too, which would help.

He came in and closed the door, for which Jamie was thankful, for the draught was making him cold again.

"Did tha' hear it?" he asked. Jack nodded. "Aye, Lad."

At that moment, Mary came down, rubbing her eyes, and had to be told. She looked at them fearfully.

"Do you think it's them Royalists again? Oh, I hope they wain't come back. It'd be the death of Mistress Jennet if she had to go through that again, an' me, too."

"N-nay, t-tis too far away. I reckon it be in P-Preston. S-sounds like a r-reet battle."

They sat and stared at each other, wondering what it could mean. Then Mary, ever practical, bestirred herself.

"Well, this'll not get t'breakfast gooing. Come on, young 'un, get them dishes on t'table. Mistress'll be waking soon and then tha can goo and wakken thi' feyther, the lazy lummock."

Mary's Lancashire accent seemed even more pronounced when she was perturbed or anxious and she was now, while she busied herself getting the morning meal ready, casting worried glances at the door of her mistress's room.

Jennet was awake, disturbed by the sounds of voices from the kitchen. She looked at the window. Why, it was broad daylight and she still in bed. She could never have lain abed like this in the old days. She was getting lazy. Putting her hand on her distended stomach, she thought, well, perhaps she had an excuse. It was not so easy these days to jump out of bed at the crack of dawn, or before. Laboriously, she struggled out of bed and began to dress. Well, soon it would be over and she would be slim again and holding her baby in her arms. It had seemed such a long, wearisome time, but it would be worth it in the end and Richard would be so pleased. She put her hand to the locket, nestling in the valley between her breasts. What was he doing now? she wondered. Suddenly, she staggered and clutched her stomach as the child gave a great lurch inside her. She fell across the bed, screaming, "Richard!"

The others rushed in at her cry and Mary gathered her in her arms. "What is it, Mistress? What's to do?" but Jennet could only sob brokenly, "He's dead. He's dead." over and over again. She moaned, bending over in agony. Mary yelled to Jack, "Quick! Run for t'midwife. It be a-coming this time for sure, and you," pointing at Jamie, "get Master Towneley. Make haste!"

The child was born in the early hours of the next morning, a boy, and at first it was thought he would not live long, so small and sickly was he. Mary, however, knew what to do. She hadn't helped to bring up so many small brothers and sisters for nothing. The child needed good, nourishing milk, and mistress could not supply that. She was gravely ill and hardly knew where she was. So Mary found a woman in the village who had a baby, just a few months old and still suckling. She prevailed upon her to come every day to feed Jennet's baby, stipulating that she should eat a good meal every day while she was with them to make the milk more nourishing. She knew what sparse fare the villagers subsisted upon. It had only been Mistress Jennet's kindness in giving Mary what she could spare in the way of food for her family that had kept them healthy, in addition to what she, Mary, gave her mother from her small wage.

After a week there was therefore, an improvement in the child's condition and he continued to thrive, to Mary's satisfaction.

Not so his mother. She lay there for weeks, sinking even deeper, rallying occasionally, to stare wildly around the room and weakly utter Richard's name. She didn't know anything when William and Henry brought Richard's body home and when he was buried in the little graveyard at Broughton Church near his grandmother. Jess was there too, buried by Master Gregson's grave.

Will had, early on brought in a physician from Preston, for the apothecary, in Will's opinion was useless. He seemed to rely, mostly, on bleeding his patients, and even to Will, that in Jennet's condition, would be fatal. She had lost a lot of blood already and had been haemorrhaging badly.

The physician examined the patient and frowned at Mistress Thomson who was there in her capacity as Nurse. She came in for a few hours each day when she was not needed anywhere else.

"Well, Sir," she asked, "what do you think? Is there any hope? The poor lass seems to be fading away. It's as though she has nothing to live for, and who could blame her? Her husband dead and all, though how she could know I know not, for no one has spoken of it before her."

He shook his head. "It is strange, I know, but I have seen many strange things in my time and often the bond between two people is so strong it defies even death to break it." He stared abstractedly. Then he said, "You say she has nothing to live for, but she has, there is the child."

He directed the midwife to prop up the sick woman against the pillows. Going to the door, he opened it and there was the village woman suckling the baby, watched by Mary.

"Bring the child in here," he ordered Mary.

"But Sir, he has not finished feeding," she protested. "T'will make him cry and disturb the mistress."

"All the better. Now place him in her arms and hold them around him. . . ."

Mary did so, wondering. The baby whimpered, his tiny mouth puckered, turning his head this way and that, searching for the nipple from which he had been so rudely snatched. Then he began to cry in earnest.

Jennet had been far away. She had been searching for Richard. Sometimes she saw him faintly and he seemed to be coming towards her, holding out his arms, but when she went forward he receded until she could not see him, only a faint spark of light, shining far away in the darkness.

She called him constantly, begging him to come back. Occasionally, he seemed to answer her but she could never quite hear what he said. She seemed to have been floating in eternity, a dot in infinite blackness.

Then a faint light appeared, getting nearer and a sound assailed her ears. What was it? The light grew brighter. It was Richard smiling, and holding something out to her. It made a sound. She was confused, wondering what it was. Richard came close, murmuring her name. He thrust the bundle into her arms and, gazing at her with love, he said one word, and then vanished from sight.

She was looking down at something cradled in her arms. It struggled and cried. Why, she thought with wonder and awe, it is my baby. Mine and Richard's.

She smiled and tightened her hold about his tiny form. He stopped crying and looked at her with the clear, unseeing gaze of the very young infant.

"Richard," she breathed happily. "Richard." What did he say? It was just one word, she remembered. Ah, yes. "LIVE!"

Yes, she would, for there was someone who needed her.

It took many weeks for Jennet to fully recover, she had been so weak. But Mary fed her nourishing broths and Will sent over plenty of milk from his own cows. And she had an incentive now, she must get well, so she could take care of young Richard. She couldn't feed him herself and she felt grieved about this, but he thrived on the foster-mother's milk and for that she must be glad.

Jennet took no interest in outside affairs, so wrapped up in the child was she. So she did not know that the Royalists, led by the Earl of Derby, lately returned from being with the King, had retaken Preston in March.

William and Henry, after burying their brother, had returned to their companies and William was with those who after taking Preston had been sent to capture Hoghton Tower from the Royalists. They had succeeded but there had been an unfortunate accident - or had it been by design? For no one knew for sure - the central tower had been blown up, killing and maiming many of their men. He counted himself lucky not to have been one of them, for hadn't he been about to cross the courtyard and go after those who had just gone up into the tower?

He had been knocked flat by the explosion, but had recovered later.

Now they were riding away from Preston, after being ordered to retreat with what forces were left. He didn't know where Henry was, but supposed he was with the foot soldiers marching behind them. Why they had allowed the Earl of Derby to recapture the town he did not know, but guessed that discretion had taken the place of valour, for the Earl had returned with far superior forces. So they were returning to Blackburn, downcast, but not defeated.

The men were grumbling, and with good cause he thought, for they, like himself, hadn't been paid for weeks, and their ammunition was now getting short. They reached their garrison at Blackburn but they were not there long before word came that Lord Derby had sacked and burned Lancaster. Reports came in also of the massacre of men, women and children.

Sir John Seaton once again marched to the relief of this town. William and Henry went too.

By this time William was beginning to feel totally disillusioned. Here they were, being moved about like pieces on a chess-board, and to what purpose? So that men like his brother could be killed or maimed for life like some of the poor wretches he had seen hobbling about on make-shift crutches, minus a leg or an arm. Why should they have to fight their own countrymen? They were not even foreigners. They spoke the same language.

Some had even been friends with those they were fighting. Brother fought brother and father fought son. It was totally, incredibly insane. "Dear God!" he prayed, "let there be an end to it!"

But there was no end, not yet. Not for a long time...

The Parliamentary forces relieved Lancaster, then were ordered to Bolton where Lord Derby was trying to take that town. He did not succeed, but believed he could take Blackburn. He called a meeting at Preston and on the 19th April was on his way up the Ribble valley to Whalley, on route to Blackburn, with a large force.

There followed the battle at Sabden Brook, near Read, where the Cavaliers were ambushed by a force of only five hundred men who shouted loud enough to make the Royalists think there were far more of them. They did not come down to face their enemy but fired from hiding, so the foe would not know how few they actually were. The Royalists fled. Lord Derby went all the way through Preston to Penwortham Priory, one of his residences, because of his shame at his army's defeat.

So Blackburn rejoiced again, and William and Henry once again were together in their garrison.

By the end of May they were in Preston again, having retaken the town. News came in thick and fast of how the Parliament was strengthening its hold on Lancashire.

Perhaps now, thought William, we may have the chance to stay here for a while and visit our home. Henry agreed. He had lost some of his earlier youthful enthusiasm for war and he needed a respite, a chance to collect his breath.

CHAPTER ELEVEN

Three years later, in 1646, on a warm sunny June day, Jennet sat in the shade of the sycamore, sewing a pinafore for her three year old son. He played at her feet, throwing up the crocheted woollen ball his mother had made for him. It was stuffed with rags, and was young Richard's most treasured toy. As she worked, Jennet's mind went back over the past three years, since that fateful spring of 1643.

After major battles and many minor skirmishes, won by first one side, then the other, Parliament had at last proved triumphant. It seemed that they could now look forward to a time of peace. Last year, though, had seen the start of the New Model Army being formed by Colonel (now General) Cromwell, and Sir Thomas Fairfax; an army well-disciplined and trained, in contrast to the rough soldiers and clubmen of previous years. Parliament wanted to send half these soldiers home, and send the rest to suppress the Irish who were again causing trouble.

But the men would have none of this. For one thing, they wanted their arrears of pay and to be assured of their future. The officers and commanders supported them, and to strengthen the position they had captured the King and held him. From being a prisoner of the Parliament, he was now the prisoner of the army.

Jennet thought of the battle of Marston Moor, the decisive battle in which the Parliament had defeated Prince Rupert, the King's nephew, in which Rupert's dog, 'Boy' had been killed. William had been in that battle, and had been sent home badly wounded. He had recovered after many months and was now at home with his wife and father. Henry was still in the army, having now attained the rank of Ensign.

And now they were at peace once more. But for how long? Jennet fervently hoped it would last. The war had done so much to her. She still felt the loss of her husband, it was like a gaping hole inside her. Thankfully, she had Richard's child. So like his father, he was. The same fair, unruly hair, and brown, straight looking, honest eyes.

She thought of that first year, how they had worked and striven just to keep alive. They had no cows to milk, so there was no cheese and butter to sell. They had used up what supplies they had saved in the store cellar, but Will had kept them going for a while. Jack and Sam ploughed up the pasture where the cows used to graze and sowed corn. Grain was in short supply, due to demand by the army, so they were able to sell it at a good price at harvest-time. Fortunately, it was a good summer for growing crops. Then when Jennet was better she had the idea of growing vegetables and herbs in her greatly enlarged garden. These helped with their own food problems, and they could sell the surplus. So they paid the rent and had a little money left to see them through the winter, if they lived very frugally. Jennet preferred not to remember that winter.

The following year, the bottom field had to lie fallow and they could not rely on that for crops, so Will had the idea of letting them have five of his twenty cows. He had been going to sell them anyway, he said, because he had lost two of his men to the army and so they were getting too much for him. They could use the bottom field to graze on as the grass came up on it. Of course, a lot of the weeds came up too, some of them injurious to cattle, as often happens on ploughed land which had not been re-sown. So they had had to set to work rooting these up before the cows could be let loose on it. Will said Jennet could pay him for the cows when she was able.

So now she and Mary could make their cheese and butter again, with the resulting buttermilk, and take them to market.

The trouble was, Jennet had thought at the time, what would they do if these, too, should be commandeered? They were fortunate, however, as the opposing forces seemed to have moved further afield, for the time being.

The shippon then had to come into use again. Sam and Jamie

didn't mind, in fact they were pleased, for in the winter the presence of five cows would considerably warm up their sleeping quarters, and there was room in the vacant stall for them. The shippon had originally been intended for six animals of which Master Gregson had had to sell one.

Jennet realised how much she owed Will Towneley, indeed, how much she owed all of them for their untiring work and loyalty, but to Will she owed the most. He had helped so much both in goods, money and time, for he came over constantly to direct the work and give helpful advice. Jack was now a competent farmworker, and with his increasing adeptness had come confidence, which in turn had helped his speech.

The stammer which had troubled him when he tried to speak was almost non-existent now, and at eighteen he was a brawny, broad shouldered youth, able to tackle most jobs on the farm. Sam, he had never quite come to trust completely, but, as they had to work constantly together, and the man seemed willing enough, there existed a sort of uneasy truce between them. Jamie was still Jack's willing slave, a fact which irked Jamie's father not a little, but he never said anything, not to Jack anyway - he was too big for that! - though to the fourteen year old Jamie, he could be cutting, especially when they were alone in the shippon at night. Jamie took it all good-naturedly; it took a lot to dispirit that lad. He had never ceased to congratulate himself on the good fortune that had brought them to Gregson's Farm, despite the hardships they had sometimes had to suffer during the past three years. Still rather small of stature, he was wiry and strong and had filled out somewhat, to Jennet's satisfaction. Mary came out just then, to tell them their midday meal was ready. Now a pretty, sensible, seventeen year old, she was devoted to her mistress and especially to the little boy. Dickon, as she called him, and now, everyone else did, too.

She called to him now, "Come, Dickon, time for dinner. Oh, you've dropped your nice ball in the puddle. What will tha mother say after she made it for thee? Look t'is all wet and dirty. Nay, don't thi cry, my bonny lad. Mary will wash it for thee."

She knelt beside the child and wiped away the tears with a corner of her pinny.

Dickon stopped crying and put chubby arms around her neck. "Wash ball, Mairly," he piped, smiling angelically. 'Mairly' was the nearest he could get to her name. He started to pull her towards the pump in the corner of the yard.

"No, Dickon, not now," said his mother, lifting him up, "dinner is ready. We will wash your ball and dry it afterwards."

"Dinner, Mammy," he repeated, as Jennet carried him into the kitchen.

Jack, Sam and Jamie came in, too, from where they were attempting to re-build the barn. They sat down thankfully.

"Ee, I be ready for this," said Jamie. " 'Tis mighty hard work we be doing lifting yon timbers. I be fair famished and me arms is coming out o' the sockets."

"Nay, thou art never owt else but famished," laughed Jack, helping himself to a large helping of mutton stew, "and as f-for hard work, tha's not seen the like. But get thi' dinner down thee, lad, and me-mebbe tha'll grow a bit, and happen in ten years time tha'll have some muscles on thee."

They all laughed, even Jamie. Jack was the only one he would allow to make jokes about his size. To anyone else he became a small bundle of fury, in keeping with his reddish hair. Neither Mary nor Jennet teased him about his stature, but the lads of the village had found out to their cost it didn't do to cross young James Grisby. It was the only thing which riled him. He so wished to be like Jack, tall and broad-shouldered, but, determined that no one should get the better of him, excepting Jack, of course, just because he was smaller than most lads of his age.

Jennet, helping Dickon with his dinner, said, " I do wish you would not tease the lad so, Jack. 'Tis not his fault he is small. Here, Dickon, eat your meat. No, don't throw your spoon down. You are a naughty boy."

"Aw 'tis only a jest, mistress. And Jamie knows it, d-don't thi' lad? Jack turned and gave Jamie a friendly cuff on the shoulder.

"Aye, Jack, 'tis only a jest," agreed the lad. "but 'tis only thee can make it, as well tha knows."

Sam grunted, resenting the hero-worship his son had for this burly young man. Mary sat silent throughout the meal, casting covert glances at Jack. It was unlike her, Jennet thought, to be so quiet. Between watching her son playing about with his dinner, and correcting him, she watched Mary's face. So that was the way of it. She had noticed several times of late how Mary had coloured up and looked away when Jack spoke directly to her. So Mary had begun to see him in a different light, had she?

Jennet was delighted. It would be ideal if her dear Mary and Jack should fall in love and marry. But sadly, it seemed to be all on Mary's side, for Jack seemed totally unaware, and took no more interest in the girl than he did in one of the cows. Indeed, Jennet felt he was far more solicitous as to the animals' welfare, than Mary's.

She would have to see what could be done, but for the moment, she had other things on her mind.

Jennet was writing a letter to her Aunt Meg that evening. She had been surprised to receive a letter from Margaret only a few months after Richard's death, for there had been no reply to the letter Richard had allowed her to write and no sign of her aunt on the few occasions she had been to Preston before the baby was born.

Afterwards she had been so ill and with no cheese and butter to sell there had been no reason to go.

Then the first letter arrived. Margaret explained that Thomas, her husband, was with the Royalist forces and refused to allow his wife to stay in Preston alone, so before Preston Guild she had gone to stay with friends of his in Cumberland. Jennet wrote back to her there, telling her of Richard's death and the birth of their son.

So, spasmodically, they had built up a correspondence between them. Jennet was sorry her aunt was so far away. It would have been nice to have had her aunt near to confide in, she would have liked to have had an older woman on whom to lean, and tell her troubles to, like the mother she barely remembered. However, these letters had to do instead.

And then, only the other day, had come the letter from her aunt telling her that Thomas was with his wife again, and with peace coming at last they were returning to Preston to take up their lives there once more. Jennet read the letter with excitement. Now she would be able to see her aunt. They would have so much to talk about and she was longing to show young Dickon to her.

Dickon. She had meant to call him Richard from the start, to keep her husband's name alive, but Mary's insistence on the diminutive and the others taking it up, too, had worn her down, and to her too he became Dickon. Besides, she reflected, Richard would be forever in her heart, so there was no need to keep reminding herself of him, and wasn't the boy the image of his father? She knew too, that in writing to, and eventually seeing, she hoped, Aunt Margaret, she was going against the wishes of both her father and husband. But they were dead, and, she believed, now knew of the folly and futility in bearing such an animosity towards others, just because of their different faith. To God, she knew in her heart, all men were the same, no matter how they chose to worship Him.

It was surprising how Jennet could have evolved such liberal views, with her strict upbringing. Perhaps it was because of it. She had, early on, begun to rebel and to look around at other people, judging them for what they were, not for what they believed in.

Only once had she felt hatred, and that was for the men who had so callously destroyed and stolen her precious things, and beaten poor Jack. She did not like to think what might have happened had they discovered Mary and herself. She had heard so many stories of how they had treated other women. And as for that so-called gentleman, that officer, Captain Standerby - she would never forget his name - how could he have allowed his men to do the things they did? He must have been as bad as they were.

There had been other soldiers who had come to the farm, both

Royalist and Parliamentarian, but most of them, seeing how poor they were, had contented themselves with what few supplies they seemed to have, leaving just a small amount for their immediate needs.

Thank God for that store cellar, she had prayed. But, at least, these other men had not burned and pillaged in wanton destruction, as Captain Standerby's men had.

It seemed to her that the soldiers who came later were beginning to tire of the constant marching and fighting. It showed in their faces.

Well, now they could go home. She hoped for their sakes they had homes to go back to, and wives and families there to welcome them. But so many would not go home . . . like Richard.

She bent over the letter. She would never get it written at this rate. When she was alone, memories had a way of crowding in on her. She looked at what she had written. "Dear Aunt Meg," was as far as she had got. She looked across at Dickon, asleep in his little bed. With a sudden resolve, she put the quill and paper away.

The day after tomorrow was market day. She would take Dickon with her and call on the Trenthams in person. It was not really polite to come unannounced, but somehow, she felt Aunt Meg would understand. Of Uncle Thomas she was not so sure, but from her aunt's letters he seemed to be a kind man.

Jennet walked down Churchgate, holding Dickon by the hand. He toddled along beside her, looking at the buildings and the crowded street with wonder. Many women passing by smiled upon the child. "Ee, my, what a bonny babby," they said. Jennet smiled back. She was proud of Dickon, with his clean gown and little apron, his shining face glowing with health, the unruly fair hair, brushed and combed. she would be glad when he was breeched though. His long gowns got so dirty, and yet she wanted to keep him like this forever, dependent on her, her own dear little baby.

Once he was breeched it would be like the first step away from her. His first step to becoming a man. But that was at least two years away yet. Some did not breech their boys until they were seven.

She had made herself as neat and tidy as possible. There was nothing to be done about her dress but it was clean and neat and the collar and cuffs were new. She still wore black, and her hair was coiled and braided under her coif as befitted a widow. Richard's locket was about her neck. She had vowed it would never leave her.

Within it now, with the lock of Richard's hair, was the little baby curl of Dickon's. She clutched the locket now, as she always did when she needed courage, for, to tell the truth, she was afraid. Afraid of what it would be like when she came face to face with Aunt Meg after so long, and Uncle Thomas too.

She neared the shop and saw there were workmen going in and out and there was scaffolding in front. A middle-aged man in good, but sober clothes seemed to be directing them. She stopped near the shop, wondering what to do. As she stood, uncertainly, the man noticed and stepped nearer, taking off his hat. He bowed.

"May I help you, Mistress?", he asked courteously. He had a low well-modulated voice and his eyes smiled, crinkling at the corners. Jennet decided she liked this man.

"Sir, I am looking for Master and Mistress Trentham," she said diffidently. "Do you know if they are at home?"

"I am Thomas Trentham, Mistress. May I enquire your name?"

"Jennet Towneley, Sir. You must be my Uncle Thomas".

He looked at her in amazement. "Jennet Towneley! Then you are the little niece my wife is always talking about."

He took her hand and kissed it. Then catching sight of Dickon peeping from behind his mother's skirts, he cried, "And who is this young gentleman? Not Master Richard, I'll be bound, he is too grown up for it to be he, for I heard he was just a babe."

Jennet smiled delightedly as Uncle Thomas held out his hand, and Dickon shyly took it. Then Master Trentham said.

"I fear you find us in a sorry state for the moment, dear niece, but no matter, Meg is within and will be as happy to see you as I am."

"Oh, Uncle, I do not wish to put you to any trouble. I can see you are busy. Mayhap, if I come another day it will be more convenient."

"Nonsense, my dear lass, I would not think of turning you away, and Meg would never forgive me. Allow me just one moment."

They were inside the shop now, and Uncle Thomas turned away to speak to a workman standing by. She looked around and saw wooden crates scattered around the shop. There were shelves all round the walls, but they were empty. Two men were busy at one end sawing and planing wood. There was a door at the back which was partly open and through it she could see what looked like a store room with more crates, and in the corner a flight of stairs.

Thomas finished speaking to the man, who then hurried away to do his bidding, and turned back to her with a smile.

"Well, my dear, let us go upstairs and give my dear wife a welcome surprise. But take care where you tread, these workmen are not over-careful where they put things."

Jennet lifted Dickon up as he ushered them through into the back room. She picked her way among the crates and tools left there by the men. Thomas indicated the stairs, and begged her leave to go up first as he wished to make the surprise announcement to his wife. When they reached the top, Jennet found they were in a small hallway with several doors leading off it, and another flight of stairs to the topmost floor of the house. Furniture cluttered the small space they were in and Jennet guessed they were still in the process of moving in. She wished now she hadn't come. They would surely not want to have a visitor at such a time.

She heard women's voices coming from one of the rooms, which seemed to be at the front. Uncle Thomas put his finger to his lips, and with an impish gleam in his eye, opened this door. He stepped inside, and greeted his wife.

"Margaret, my dear, I. . . ."

"Oh, Tom, there you are. Come here, will you and help us with these curtains? Sarah, be careful, girl, you will have them down again. No, not that way! I declare girl, you have no sense at all."

Thomas tried again to attract his wife's attention.

"Margaret! Will you listen? I - I have brought a very important visitor to see you. Leave those curtains alone and come and greet her."

"Oh Tom, you haven't! Who is it? Oh my, and me looking like this, and the house in such a state!"

He motioned to Jennet to come into the room. She set the child down and taking his hand, advanced nervously.

She found herself in a large, sunlit room, somewhat untidy, with furniture set at odd angles evidently waiting to be arranged in its proper place. There were fabrics strewn over a large sideboard, and on chairs. A young girl was standing on a stool holding up a length of curtain and Aunt Margaret was hastily smoothing her hair, and attempting to undo the strings of a capacious apron all at the same time. She looked flustered, and faintly annoyed, but when she saw who it was her plumpish features broke into a welcoming smile.

"Jennet! It's my dear little niece! Oh Tom, you scallywag. Why didn't you say who it was? Let me look at you. Why you have grown into a beauty!"

She embraced her niece effusively, talking rapidly all the time. when she could get a word in, Jennet began to apologise for her untimely intrusion.

"Aunt Meg, I am indeed sorry to come at such a time. You must be. . . ."

"Nay lass, do not be sorry. I am so happy to see you. But I do wish we were in better order, I must admit. Oh, what am I thinking of? Here, Sarah, clear a chair and place it for Mistress. . . ."

Here Dickon, having found himself ignored, and with these strange people fussing around his mother set up a howl of indignation. Jennet sat down in the ornate brocade chair the maid hastily set for her and gathered Dickon up, hushing him.

Margaret held up her hands in pity. "Oh the poor lamb! Was no one noticing you, then? What a shame. Come Tom, help me get some order here, and you, Sarah, fetch a glass of wine and some cakes, and a cup of milk for the little one."

Tom and Margaret bustled round clearing the room. They found a small table and brought it to the centre of the room and set chairs round it. Sarah came in with a tray on which was a bottle of wine and three glasses, a plate of tiny cakes and biscuits, and a china cup of milk. They sat down and Tom poured out the wine and handed a glass to Jennet. Dickon had stopped crying and had buried his face in his mother's neck. She took a sip of wine and replaced the glass carefully on the table. They were beautiful, expensive looking glasses, and the china cup had a nosegay of roses painted on it. It looked so fragile and lovely, she thought it was too dainty for the likes of them, if Dickon should break it! She would die of shame.

But Margaret was pressing a biscuit upon the child. She coaxed him and presently, he peeped out and seeing the sugared confection so temptingly held before him, put out his hand. Margaret drew it back and said in a wheedling tone, "Come, my little man, come to Aunt Meg and you shall have the biscuit."

His little face puckered up for an instant, as though he was about to cry again, but Meg enticed him and then drew him up on to her lap. With the biscuit clutched in his chubby hand, he took and bite and, chewing ecstatically, beamed upon them all.

Jennet heaved a sigh of relief and nibbled at the cake offered to her by Tom, it was delicious. And now, there was Meg holding the cup of milk to the child's lips. He drank thirstily and tried to hold it as she drew it away.

"Pitty," he gurgled, "pitty fower." They all laughed, and then started talking all at once. Soon Jennet found herself telling her Aunt and Uncle of the farm and how they had fared, during those difficult years, all the things she had not been able to say in her letters.

They, in turn, spoke of their experiences and Jennet was enthralled. But, after an hour, when the carved clock on the mantel struck three, she rose, with apologies, saying she must go, having left Mary and Jamie at the Market-place.

Meg exclaimed at this, saying Jennet should have brought them, too. So she explained that they had to be left to sell the produce.

"Then," said Meg, "when we are settled you must fetch them, I would like to see Jack especially, the brave lad, and, of course, Mary, who has stayed with you so loyally, your father-in-law, too. He must be a good man. Mayhap I could come and pay you all a visit one day?"

So saying, she ushered Jennet down the stairs and through the shop, Thomas following.

"When this is finished you will see a difference. All these crates contain my books, soon to be on these shelves. There was some damage done during the war, but we are slowly coming to rights, my dear."

He and Meg kissed her and little Dickon, and she went through the door into the sunny afternoon.

She turned to wave to them as they stood in the doorway, and as she turned back almost collided with a dark, tallish man walking towards the shop. He put out his hand, and steadied her as she stumbled.

"My apologies, Mistress," he said, taking off his hat and making a deep bow. She looked into a pair of dark blue, almost violet eyes, with a faintly mocking gleam in them. His dark hair was down to his shoulders, curling at the ends and his long moustache gave him an arrogant sardonic air. A cavalier, she thought, if ever I saw one, though how she knew this she couldn't tell, for he did not wear the elaborate dress she was accustomed to think they wore. No, he was attired in much the same sort of clothes as her Uncle Tom.

Thinking about it on the way home, she thought it was because they did not wish to be conspicuous in these victorious Parliamentary times. Royalists were still looked on with suspicion. But who was this man? He looked as if he was a friend of the Trenthams, for she had turned round quickly as she went up the street, and had seen him being greeted by them with cordiality.

In bed that night she could not stop thinking about the visit to her aunt and uncle. Going over their conversation, she thought of things she should have said, and things she should not. But it was no use going over that. It was over and done with and couldn't be changed. She was glad, though, she had gone. They were so kind and had bidden her to dinner next week, when they hoped the house, at least, would be more habitable.

And always her thoughts returned to the dark man who had bumped into her, or rather, whom she had bumped into. She was filled with speculation about him, wondering who he was. There was something about him that was familiar. She could not think what it was. And there was that strange feeling on her arm where he had gripped it, a sort of tingling sensation. She could still feel it. She rubbed her arm, still wondering, and drifted off to sleep, to dream of strange, dark men, gripping her arm and threatening her in menacing tones.

CHAPTER TWELVE

The next week saw Jennet arriving early at the Trenthams. It was a hot, muggy day, with a hint of rain in the grey clouds massing overhead, so she had brought her dark cloak over her arm, and was wishing she hadn't, for her arm felt hot and sticky under its heavy folds.

She looked at the Parish Church clock. Almost one o'clock, she was on time. She never passed the Parish Church without thinking of that day nearly four years ago when she and Richard had come to Preston Guild and they had watched the colourful procession emerge from its doors and pass through the town. So much had happened since then, but that was one day she would never forget.

She came to the shop. The scaffolding had gone, the windows were unshuttered and the glass shone. The shop had been painted, and looked clean and fresh. The door was open, so she entered to see the shelves were now filled with books, all kinds of books. She longed to browse through them; perhaps Uncle Tom would let her sometime. So many thousands of words written painstakingly by learned men. It was awe-inspiring.

Uncle Tom was behind the counter serving a customer. He smiled and greeted her, and requested her to go on upstairs. She curtsied to him and his customer and went through into the back room and up the stairs.

Aunt Meg came forward as she entered the room, and embraced her. She looked surprised at finding her alone.

"Did you not bring your friends, Jennet" she asked, "and the little Dickon? I declare, I am disappointed, he is such a lovely child."

Jennet had to make excuses. "I am afraid they are unused to fine company, as indeed I am myself, and could not be persuaded to attend, but they send their apologies and greetings, and many thanks for your kind invitation. Dickon I did not bring because he can be troublesome at meal times and I would not have him throw his dinner on to your beautiful carpet."

Meg laughed, "Oh, I am sure he cannot be like that, he looked so angelic, such a darling."

"You do not know him, Aunt." Jennet looked around her as the maid-servant took her cloak and her aunt begged her to be seated. The room looked so different now. The curtains of dark red velvet gave the room an opulent look. The crimson patterned carpet went beautifully with them. There was no fire lit in the fireplace. It was too warm for that, but there was a large Chinese vase filled with flowers in its place. Bookshelves along one wall were filled with books. 'More books!' she thought. The chair she sat in was padded and comfortable. Margaret sat in another like it.

"This room is the most beautiful one I have ever seen." She had not seen many it was true, she thought.

"I am glad, Aunt Meg, that I did not bring Dickon," she went on, looking at the carpet. Meg said, "But we do not eat in here, my dear. We shall move into the dining-room when our other guest arrives. He is late." She looked at the clock, "It is already fifteen minutes past the hour."

Jennet smiled to hide her confusion. She had been wondering where the table was if they were to eat in here. There was only the small table near her aunt's chair and that was not very adequate. So they ate in another room? She was so used to farm life where the big kitchen was dining-room, living room and kitchen, even bedroom since Jack had taken to sleeping there. True, with a surprising talent for carpentry he had turned the alcove into a box-bed, and Mary had made curtains to disguise it.

She felt more than ever like a country cousin. Then another thought struck her. She had hardly been listening when her aunt had mentioned the other guest, but now she realised what Meg had said. 'The other guest', and a man, too. Oh dear, what ever was she going to do? She was sure she would disgrace herself, and her aunt and uncle too, by her country manners - or lack of them.

Then there were voices on the stairs and footsteps ascending. She felt panicky and fought to control herself. Now they were in the room, Uncle Thomas and another man. It was the same man she had collided with in the street. He was dressed now in a dark green velvet coat with a wide lace collar, and had evidently worn a cloak which he had taken off downstairs. He surrendered this, with his hat, to Sarah, the maid, and came forward, bowing to Jennet as Thomas introduced them. She rose and curtsied.

"Jennet, may I present Master Roger Standerby, lately Major Standerby, one of my oldest friends?" The man took her hand, bowing, and kissed it. Again she felt that odd tingling feeling but was hardly aware, she was frozen in space, a fixed smile on her face. Thomas was still talking, but she didn't hear. That name was whirling round in her head. Roger Standerby! STANDERBY! He had been a captain then, yes and hadn't her father-in-law mentioned that he had told him his name was Roger? Yes it was. Roger Standerby. *Captain* Roger Standerby. No doubt he had won promotion to Major. No wonder she had thought there was something familiar about him, it was his voice, the voice she had heard just seconds before she had fainted, and only moments later his men had set fire to the barn and beaten Jack to within an inch of his life. She felt sick and thought she was going to faint. She swayed. Roger Standerby caught her and asked solicitously, "Are you ill, Mistress?"

Tom fussed about her, sitting her in the chair again and Meg looked around helplessly, calling for Sarah.

"It is the heat, poor girl." said Tom, fanning her.

"I - I am alright," she managed to say, forcing herself to be calm. For her aunt and uncle's sake she must not show her repugnance for their guest. "It is nothing, just a little dizziness."

"You are sure, Jennet?" asked her Aunt, "I will have Sarah bring cool water for you to bathe your face and hands."

The maid had come in looking anxious, but Jennet said firmly, "No, thank you Aunt, I do assure you, I am better now. I am sorry to cause such trouble. It was, as you say, just the heat."

She stood up to prove it, and Uncle Tom went quickly towards her in case she should fall, but she did not, and he, obviously relieved, said. "Then shall we go in to our meal? Mayhap the food and a glass of wine will help to dispel the vapours, my dear niece."

He took her arm and led her towards the other room, her aunt following with Master Standerby.

She found herself in a room slightly larger than the front room, a room strangely familiar. The large oaken table in the centre covered with a white cloth, had silver dishes on it. The walls were hung with tapestries and there was a sideboard, also in oak, highly polished. There was no fire in the grate, but, as in the other room, a vase held sweet smelling flowers and herbs to hide its emptiness. It looked liked the room she had seen in her dreams, it seemed so long ago, and which she had never forgotten. When they were seated at one end of the long table, she remembered the nebulous figure she had also seen. It must be Uncle Tom, she thought, it could never be that odious man, now sitting opposite her. She tried not to look at him, but she had to reply to his questions as to her welfare and her home. She answered coldly and in monosyllables and soon, looking puzzled, he shrugged slightly and gave up, concentrating all his attention on his host and hostess.

Aunt Meg prattled on, explaining how when Tom had joined the army, and she had gone to stay in Cumberland, all their furniture and goods had been packed up and stored with an old friend who lived in Cheshire, in a fortified manor.

"Else we might not have had anything left to come back to," she confided to Jennet, "the looting and pillaging that went on were terrible. No one was safe, as you well know, my dear."

Jennet kept her eyes on her food. Of course, Aunt Meg knew of their misfortunes at the farm. She had written to her of it, but had not divulged the name of the Royalist officer who was responsible. She wished now she had, then she would have been spared this meeting with that monster. Her aunt and uncle would surely not have invited him when she was there.

Roger Standerby began to talk of the war and of the King, but

Uncle Tom tactfully steered him away from the subject, looking sympathetically at Jennet.

"Come Roger, let us not embroil ourselves with politics. The ladies, I am sure, prefer to talk of more pleasant things."

So it went on. And on. Jennet never knew how she got through that meal. She did not know what she ate, but it was not much. She picked at the food, until her Aunt noticed and asked if she was still feeling unwell.

"Oh no, Aunt, I am perfectly well. It is just that I am not very hungry, but the food is delicious. I am indeed sorry that I cannot do more justice to your excellent cooking. Yes, perhaps I can manage just a little of that syllabub, it looks so inviting."

She accepted the dish that her Aunt proffered to her and tried to apply herself to it, but every mouthful seemed to choke her. At last it was over and they rose from the table and retired to the other room, while the maid began to clear away the dishes.

As soon as she decently could, Jennet declared she must be going as she had left Jack waiting with the wain and she was sure Dickon would be proving troublesome with Mary, back at the farm. She knew this would not be so, as Dickon was devoted to his 'Mairly' and that young lady was quite capable of dealing with him, if he should prove so. But she had to get away, away from Master Standerby and his disturbing presence.

He offered to accompany her back to where Jack was waiting but she hurriedly brushed his offer aside, declaring it was not far, and she could not possibly trouble him for so small a distance.

She took her leave, kissing her aunt and uncle and with a stiff curtsy to Master Standerby. They pressed her to come again soon, her aunt saying she expected to see her at Market, and would tell her of the next occasion when they would be entertaining. She made an excuse, saying they would be very busy during the next few moths what with the hay making and then the harvest.

Meg brushed this aside with an airy wave of the hand. "But of course you can spare an hour or two to visit us. I will not do without your company now that we have been re-united."

It was no use. They would not listen, but she was determined not to come there again, while Roger Standerby was likely to be there. He looked as though he might be a frequent visitor, too. He seemed to be on such excellent and cordial terms with them.

She hurried up Churchgate, past the Bull where she had heard Master Standerby say he was staying while in Preston, not turning round to wave to them as they stood in the shop doorway for she knew he was still with them, and soon she was in the Market-place, where Jack was waiting.

He noticed her look of distress and asked what was the matter. She made a non-committal answer and climbed into the cart.

She was silent and preoccupied all the way home and Jack cast frequent concerned glances at her, but forbore to ask her again what ailed her. Something had upset her, for sure, and it was a shame; she had so looked forward to visiting her aunt and uncle again, he knew. She had talked of nothing else all week. Mayhap, he should have gone with her, as she said he had been invited, but he knew that he could never have fitted in with her grand relations with his rough country clothes and speech. He thought that he and Mary had only been included in the invitation out of politeness, for he knew how Jennet had spoken of them with affection as her friends, not as servants. But, nothing could alter the fact that they were indeed, just that, servants, and nothing more, despite what she said, and as such, could not expect to be welcomed as equals. It was not in nature, mused Jack, for Master or Mistress and servants to mix in polite society.

CHAPTER THIRTEEN

During the next few months, Jennet fended off all attempts by her Aunt to entice her into visiting them. She stopped going to Preston Market, sending Mary instead. She told the girl that it was time she took over the job, as it would help her to meet people and broaden her outlook. It was a lame excuse, but Mary took it at its face value and was not averse. She liked the bustling life of the town, and had been there on the few occasions when Jennet could not go. So it became her permanent task. Aunt Meg wrote several letters begging her to come, to which Jennet replied evasively, saying she was busy and they had so much to do on the farm.

Once, Mary came back from market saying she had been approached by a lady who said she was Jennet's Aunt Margaret, and would she ask her Mistress to call and see her. The lady, Mary said, had been accompanied by two gentlemen, one probably her husband. He was much older and more soberly dressed than the other, who seemed about thirty years old.

So he was still around, thought Jennet. She had hoped he might be away. Did he not have estates or business of his own to attend to? Times when he would not have to be in Preston, and she could, with safety, visit her relations.

Mary was asking her if she would be calling on her aunt, and if there was any message she could give her, if she should see her again at the market. She seemed a nice lady, too, and so kind.

"No," said her Mistress, "just say I am busy and thank her."

Mary was puzzled. What had come over Mistress Jennet lately? She was not at all her usual self. She seemed to have changed since - yes - since that day she had gone to dinner with her Aunt and Uncle. They had all plied her with questions on her return, expecting her to be excited and happy and eager to talk about it. Instead, she had been morose and preoccupied, refusing to say anything. It was very strange, her sudden reversal of attitude towards her aunt. They all knew how she had longed to re-establish friendly relations with her.

Mary was not a deep-thinker, but she was not unintelligent. Despite her simple upbringing and lack of education, she was able to put two and two together and had a native wit. She was not really fooled by Jennet's reasons for sending her, Mary, to Preston instead of going herself. She knew how her Mistress had enjoyed her trips to the town, previously. So she had done her bidding, concluding that something had happened at her aunt and uncle's house which had completely upset Jennet, and she tried as best she could to find out, but with no success. . . .

It was a pity, she thought , that such a lovely young woman as Jennet would have cut herself off from her only relations, and had no friends except Master Towneley and his sons, and her own immediate household. She should have a husband, she was young enough to have a large family yet. But where was she to find a husband in her restricted circle?

Mary sighed, and gave up her speculations, and hurried off to the dairy to get on with her cheese-making.

Jennet threw herself into her work on the farm and in looking after her son. Only by completely occupying herself every minute could she forget that man. But there were some tasks which occupied only her hands, and were so familiar that she could do them almost without thinking, when her mind wandered and try as she might to think of other things, her thoughts invariably came back to Roger Standerby.

How she hated him! She hated his arrogance, his mocking glance, his utter disregard for the feelings of others. There was no humanity in him, he was selfish, cruel and utterly evil. At times like this, her feelings were such that her hands clenched, her eyes flashed fire. She would love to have him helpless and at her mercy. What wouldn't she like to do to him to take revenge for all those others to whom, she had no doubt, he had caused anguish and suffering, just as he had done to the inhabitants of Gregson's Farm. She nursed her hate, feeling it grow inside her like a cancer.

Mary and Jack watched her with concern. Even Will sensed something was happening to his daughter-in-law and gazed at her in puzzlement. He spoke to William about it, but he could not account for it either. Jennet did not go often to Whitegate Farm. Alice was now the Mistress, to Will's despair, and poor William was completely under her thumb. Jennet did not like what she had done to William and what she was doing to Will, he was looking old and weary lately, and worried, too. Alice was extravagant and money ran through her hands like water. She liked to dress grandly and ape her betters and refused to spoil her pretty hands with household tasks. So, everything was left to servants, who were not always as careful as they should be.

Jennet longed to help, but it would not do to interfere in someone else's household, especially when the household was the domain of someone like Alice. So she kept away, but made Will and William welcome whenever they came to visit. Alice did not come, she felt herself above visiting their poor neighbours, as she termed them.

So, the year went on, and Christmas came again and passed, and then they were in a New Year.

Sixteen-forty-seven! And here was her birthday again. She was twenty-two. Not a great age, but she felt as if she had lived through several life-times. The others gave her little gifts, which she accepted gratefully. Will did not come, but towards the end of the afternoon William arrived looking pale and unhappy.

He greeted her with a kiss, and wished her well on her birthday. She thanked him gravely and, seeing his distracted air, asked what was amiss.

He hesitated a moment, then said, "It is my Father, Jennet, he is sick. For months now he has been ailing, getting steadily worse, but would not allow himself to succumb. Now he has taken to his bed and I fear will never leave it. He is in great pain, too. Oh, sister Jennet, I do not know what to do!"

He covered his face with his hands. Jennet cried out in shock at his words. Then she asked, "Will Alice mind if I come to nurse him?"

He caught her hands in gratitude, "Oh, would you? I was hoping you would, but feared to ask. Alice will not go near him. She has lately conceived and says she fears to put the child in jeopardy by going where there is sickness. The physician says there is no hope."

She found herself giving brisk orders to Mary and Jack. Jack was to have complete control of the farm while she was away, for she meant to stay with Will while he needed her. To Mary she gave charge of Dickon and the house and dairy. To Will she owed a debt of gratitude she could never repay but she meant to discharge a little of that debt in caring for this man who had done so much for her.

They buried him on a blustery March day, while the clouds scudded across a pale blue sky. Jennet stood with William beside the grave, while the parson intoned words which had no meaning for her. The servants and farm-hands clustered round them, as well as one or two distant relations of the Towneleys whom Jennet did not know. Henry was there, too, looking grim-faced, and so much older than his years. Alice had stayed at home, claiming her pregnancy was making her unwell, and she did not think a funeral would be conducive to the unborn child's wellbeing. Nobody argued with her, it was easier and more peaceful to say nothing.

About a week after the funeral, William came with startling news. He and Alice were leaving Whitegate Farm.

"I do not feel that I can go on farming", he told her diffidently, "my heart is no longer in it, and for some time it has not shown a profit. My father worked himself to death in it. Alice has persuaded me to go to Goosnargh and work with her father who is getting on in years and needs help. The mill is a prosperous one and will be mine when he goes. I must also think of Alice and the child."

Jennet could almost hear Alice speaking. She knew how William's wife had hated the farm life, and, she thought, if that lazy, selfish young woman had lived a little more frugally and buckled to with the work as a farmer's wife should, it might still have been as prosperous as it had been in Granny Towneley's time.

But she could not say these things to William. Despite her faults, he loved his wife.

"I shall miss you, William," she said sadly, "and the debt I owed your father for the cows will be paid to you."

She had saved a little each week out of her earnings with the dairy produce and had been paying off her debt to Will but there was still some money owing.

"My father talked to me privily on his death-bed about this. He said that you were not to pay anything more. The debt is finished, and, as the stock and equipment are to be sold, you are to come and take what you want, first."

"Oh William! This is not right. Anything I owed your father should now be paid to you. You are his heir."

"No, Jennet my dear sister. It was his dying wish, and it is also my wish. You deserve more for what you did to ease his last days."

"William, I owed a debt to your father that can never be repaid. His unfailing help and generosity was the only thing that saved us during those terrible days after Richard died, and I can never forget how he rushed over to save us when those men set fire to the barn."

"Aye, he was a good man", William said, "it is a pity one does not recognise the worth in one's parents until they are gone. I was never the most helpful of his sons, I - I never really wanted to be a farmer and he knew it. Would to God it had been Richard who had lived."

He brushed a hand across his eyes. "Aye, Richard was the one who should have been his heir. He loved the land, but I could only think of the difficulties. How one is subject to the weather and whether the cattle may fall sick or their milk run dry."

"But all farmers have these fears, William, and Richard as much as any. He often used to despair of getting the crop in on time and whether the effort was worth it in the long run. 'Tis a common thing among farmers.

"I know, but with me it was different. But let us not waste time in bewailing what cannot now be changed. You are having trouble in rebuilding your barn, are you not?"

"Yes, it is true. It is taking a long time because we are short of timber and Jack and Sam cannot spare much of their time away from their ordinary work. Jamie tries to help, but he is too young to be able to do much."

"Then let me help. It is the least I can do. My men have not needed to do much farm work this spring. I have told them I will not be working the farm and was going to send them off. They will not be at a loss for I have arranged for them to find work on other farms. So, until we leave I will send them over to help re-build your barn, and as we have wood in plenty which is not needed, they will bring that, too. You shall also have what livestock you need and any other equipment."

Jennet was overwhelmed. She tried to thank her brother-in-law but he would have none of it. It was his duty, he said, to help his dear sister-in-law, who was like the real sister he never had.

"My Father loved you too, you know. He told me once that he would have married you when your father lay dying, but Master Gregson would not hear of it. Your father did not think it right. Afterwards, he realised the truth of it, and was glad it was Richard, for he looked on you as a daughter and loved you as such."

"Yes, it was true," Jennet said, "no Father could have done more for me. But I, too, am glad it was Richard, though we had such a short time together, for we loved each other well and I am glad too, that it brought me such a brother as you."

She flung her arms around him and kissed him on the cheek, overcome with emotion. They clung together for a moment, before he made his farewells and left.

It was May before the business of Whitegate Farm was wound up. Everything movable was sold, but not before William had sent over three more cows and some pigs and chickens. He had also been true to his word in having his men come over with carts of wood and tools, to finish the barn. The shippon had to be enlarged to accommodate the extra stock. She also received some dairy equipment, which was badly needed. William asked her, too, to come over to the house to select any furniture she required. She was diffident about this, fearing Alice would not be pleased.

"It is Alice who has suggested it," he assured her, "we shall not need it all, and what is left will have to be disposed of."

So Jennet went, and found Alice much more affable, although a trifle condescending. She suspected it was because Alice was getting her own way and leaving the farm she detested, or perhaps her approaching motherhood had mellowed her, although Jennet had her doubts about that.

She found Alice reclining gracefully on a sofa in the parlour. She had often wished that there had been another room like this at her own home, somewhere where she could retire to be alone, or to receive visitors in. Not that she had many visitors of course, but it would have been nice, just the same.

Alice rose and extended her hand languidly.

"My dear Jennet," she said, in affected tones, "so you have come to pick out some furniture, though I vow, 'tis not worth the having. So old fashioned, all of it. But, mayhap you will find it useful, though, how you will fit even just one piece into that small house of yours, I do not know. I have often wondered why you have not extended the farmhouse. William's father did that to this house, many years ago, and my own father is even now having an extension built on the the Mill-house to accommodate us."

She smoothed the lilac gown over her stomach which was just beginning to show in a rounded curve.

"Yes," replied Jennet, "I am afraid there is not much room, I will admit. I have often wished to have more space, and it is true that I will not be able to take more than one piece. A table perhaps, or a chest? Or if you have a small bed for Mary's room. I should like her to have a decent bed."

"It is not good to spoil servants, my dear," said Alice, leading the way into the yard. She picked her way daintily through the muddy patches, holding up her skirts. "We have put all the furniture we do not want into the barn, so you can select it at your leisure. William is in there, talking to a gentleman who has come to buy some goods."

She called to her husband through the open door. He came out with a florid-faced gentleman in country clothes, evidently a farmer. The man raised his hat to them and bowed, then went away on his horse which had been tethered in a corner of the yard.

Alice said, "Here is Jennet come to pick some furniture for her little house, Husband. I have just been telling her, she should think of building another wing to house it all. But, I declare, this cold air is getting to me. I will return to the house and get some refreshment made ready for you when you have concluded your business." She returned to the house, shivering ostentatiously, and hurried inside.

William watched his wife fondly, and then turned to Jennet.

"I fear my wife feels the cold greatly, though I confess I think it is quite warm today, but the wind is strong certainly. Now, my dear, shall we inspect the furniture?"

He conducted her inside the large barn, and Jennet saw many items of furniture scattered about among the bales of straw and hay and sacks of meal.

She exclaimed over the solid oak sideboard and the teak chests, and there were several elegant tables and chairs, all much too good for her little house, she thought, but there was a good, big kitchen table, much better than their own, and some beds, solidly made, with mattresses.

"William, I confess I would like it all. It is so lovely, all of it, but there is no room, and much of it is too grand for us, so perhaps I may just take the kitchen table and a bed for Mary and, yes, a chest and one chair for my own bed-chamber."

William was looking at her in a speculative way and she quailed inside. Perhaps she had asked for too much, she did not want him to think her greedy, and he had already given her so much.

"Oh Will!" she cried, "Am I being too presumptuous? I will just take the bed then, for Mary, who has to sleep on that hard pallet!"

"Nay lass," he laughed, "I have just been thinking, Alice is right, you should have them all. There. . . ."

"But where can I put it?" she interrupted, in her eagerness, "there is little enough room as it is."

William put up his hand to silence her. "Now, will you let me finish? I was going to say - there is a cottage, built by my Father, which does not belong to the farm. It is vacant now, and is built of stone. Why should we not dismantle it, and take the stones over to your farm and build an extension on to the house? Then you can have a parlour and some extra chambers in which to put all this, and in the meantime, now that the barn is finished you can store it there. I do not have to vacate this place until the end of June, so that will give me time to supervise the dismantling of the cottage and perhaps to see the start of the rebuilding. What do you say to that? Are you agreeable?"

Jennet was unable to speak for a few moments, she was so thunderstruck. She had stood there while William spoke, unable to grasp what he was saying at first. Then her face broke into a smile.

"William, you cannot mean it! It is so wondrous, I cannot believe it could happen. Is it really possible? I have wished so many times that we had a larger house, but . . ." her face fell as a sudden thought struck, "It will take a great deal of money to do all this, surely. There will be mortar to buy and the men to pay for their work, and oh, many other things. Things which I know nought about."

"There is one other thing which I have to tell you." William paused a moment as though he was considering his words. "My Father, as you know, was a frugal man, all his life. He liked to save as much as possible. During the years when the farm was more prosperous he saved quite a fair amount, but lately it has not been so much. Still, it amounted to quite a good sum in the end. He had left instructions that it was to be divided equally between Richard, Henry and me. When Richard was killed, it was to go to you. Henry has had his share and has gone back to his garrison in Manchester. I hear he has betrothed himself to a rich merchant's daughter and intends to settle there. I have received mine, and yours will be given to you by Father's lawyer as soon as you can get into Preston to sign the papers."

"H'how much is it?" asked Jennet breathlessly. "Will it be enough to pay for the building?"

"About two hundred pounds. That should be more than enough. Now shall we go into the house? I can see Alice signalling through the window for us to go in for our refreshment. But give me a moment to instruct the men to load this furniture on to a wagon."

Jennet rode home on the wain, loaded with her new furniture. She was in a dream, in which she saw her home transformed. Soon it would be a reality. If only - if only Richard had been here to see it. And once again she had to feel gratitude towards her father-in-law and, of course, to William. What good friends had the Towneleys proved themselves to be. To think that only a few short years ago they had been virtually strangers, just the people living on the next farm, due to her Father's insistence on their keeping themselves to themselves and not becoming too intimate with their neighbours.

But he had had to accept their help in he end, hadn't he? And through that, all this had come about. It showed that one should never be too proud to accept help when it is freely offered, and never to assume that strangers are not good, honest and generous people underneath, as many people she had met had proved.

All except one, and he could never be other than she imagined him to be. She had proof enough of that.

Jennet said farewell to William at the end of June. It was an emotional scene, her heart was full, there was so much she wanted to say, but could not find the words to adequately express it. She wept openly, and William tried to laugh her out of it, possibly to hide the tears that were in his own eyes.

"Come now, Sister, I am not going to the end of the world. Goosnargh is only a mile or two away and there will be many times when we can visit each other. When Alice is delivered she will want you to see the child. We will meet, just you see."

Jennet did not feel she would see him again. Alice, who had already gone on to her Father's, declaring she would not stay in this place another minute, would surely see to that, no matter what he said.

So off he went, but as he was riding out of the gate, Jennet ran quickly forward and took his hand, and kissing it, whispered a fervent, "Thank you."

She felt as though a chapter in her life had come to an end. Her father had gone and poor old Jess, Richard and Will and now William. Henry would never come back, either. So it was all finished.

But when she turned around, wiping the tears from her eyes, and saw how the addition to the house was progressing; looked at the new barn, and the much larger shippon, and the extra animals which had been added to their stock, she thought perhaps a new chapter was only just beginning.

CHAPTER FOURTEEN

Mary was troubled. She had something to tell her Mistress which she feared might upset her. It was all to do with whatever it was that had caused the rift between her and her Aunt. At least, it seemed to be all on Mistress Jennet's side, not her Aunt's, for that poor lady had tried so hard to maintain their good relations. Mary wished she knew what it was and how she could help. If she told her Mistress, then she might go into one of those irritable moods, but if she said nothing and Mistress found out, then she would be in trouble. It was so difficult to know what to do. Sometimes she wished Mistress Jennet had not gone to see her Aunt in the first place. But things had been a little better since Master Towneley died, poor man. For her Mistress had had so much on her mind, it seemed, that whatever had been troubling her had been pushed into the background. She knew Jennet was sad over Master Will's death, and then Master William leaving, but the excitement over the changes in the house and farm had taken up all her time and attention. Now that everything had settled down, she hoped that Mistress would be happier in her mind.

So she hesitated to say anything lest she should upset her Mistress again, but events took their own turn.

It was in September, when Mary and Jennet were in the dairy shaping the pats of butter and cutting the cheeses and wrapping them carefully for market.

Mary heard it first. It was the sound of carriage wheels coming into the yard. She went pale - surely it couldn't be - but it must be, for she had heard carriage wheels twice before, and only one person she knew had ever come to the farm in a carriage. It was certainly not the farm wagon. It was lighter than that. Jennet hadn't heard it. She was too engrossed in banging the pats of butter into shape.

Mary went to the door and opened it. She saw the lady descending from the light carriage.

She turned, her throat dry, but managed to croak, "Mistress-Mistress Jennet," in a harsh whisper.

Jennet looked up just then, although she hadn't heard Mary's low voice. "What is it, Mary? You look as if you'd seen a ghost. Is someone there?"

Mary swallowed; then managed to find her voice.

"I think it's your Aunt, Mistress, come to visit."

Jennet stood stock still, her face pale and distraught. But in a minute she pulled herself together and, smoothing her dress and cap and tucking the stray tendrils of hair into place, she went to the door. There in the yard was the small carriage, and the horse standing held by the driver. Her Aunt was looking uncertainly about her.

Jennet went forward. "Good day, Aunt," she managed to say. Margaret stood looking at her, a strange look on her face. Then she faltered a few steps, holding out her arms, and enveloped her niece.

Mary was in the kitchen, giving the coachman a cup of ale and a bite to eat, while Margaret and Jennet were in the new parlour. She had been told by her Mistress to take in a glass of their carefully hoarded wine and some biscuits, in a few minutes. Dickon sat on the floor near the fire, gazing solemnly at the man, and clutching his precious ball, now looking sadly the worse for wear. Mary was worried: now it would come out, how Mistress Trentham had come earlier in the year when Mistress Jennet was over at Whitegate Farm nursing Master Will. She had come again, the day when Jennet was again at the Towneleys to get her furniture. Mary had put her off the second time, saying her Mistress might be away all day. Well, it was partly true. *She* did not know how long Jennet was going to be. She might have told her when she returned, but Jennet was so full of joy with her new furniture and her plans for the house, she hadn't the heart to spoil it. Now, she didn't know what would happen. She picked up the tray with the glasses of wine and biscuits, and went over to the newly-made door into the parlour and knocked on it. Inside, she found the two ladies sitting near the small table in the centre, on two of the elegant chairs William had given to Jennet. The oak sideboard and one of the teak chests were there, too, and wonder of wonders, a small green carpet, given specially by William to round off the room, was placed in front of the small fireplace. Of course, Jennet admitted, the stone walls needed something to cover their bareness, but she hoped to remedy that as soon as she could.

Mary put the tray on the table, curtsied and left the room. She was full of curiosity, but there was nothing in either of the two ladies' faces to tell her anything. Aunt Meg had been talking, but stopped when Mary entered. Jennet sat stiffly, staring in front of her.

Back in the kitchen, Mary found young Dickon standing by the driver's chair, showing him his ball. The man, a kind faced middle-aged fellow, examined it carefully.

"Well, that is a bonny ball, my young Master" he said gravely, "Who made it for thee?"

"Mammy," said Dickon, smiling, and proceeded to climb on to the man's knee.

"Nay, Dickon," said Mary, "you must not trouble the poor man like that. Get you down this minute."

The driver laughed, "Let the young Master be, Mistress. I've had young 'uns of my own, though they be all grown up now and gone." He added this last a trifle wistfully.

So Mary forgot her fears, talking to the driver, and watching fondly as Dickon chattered away to his new friend.

"But Jennet," Margaret was saying, a pleading note in her voice, "why won't you tell me why it is that you have kept refusing to see us? Have we offended you? I have tried so many times to see you. When you stopped coming to Preston market I thought you were ill, and I was so worried. Then one of the market women pointed out your maid and said she was coming in your place, so I spoke to her and asked how you were. She replied that you were well, but that you were now busily occupied in looking after Dickon and the farm, but I asked her to give you a message to come and see me. I waited for weeks, but you never came. When I wrote to you, all I received were stiff little letters telling me you were too busy."

"It was true, Aunt," said Jennet, "and then I was nursing my poor father-in-law until he died. Since then, I have had to supervise the building of this extension to the house, which was all brought about by the generosity of by brother-in-law, who has now left to live at Goosnargh with his wife."

"Yes, I heard about your father-in-law's illness, but I am sorry to hear that he is dead. He must have been a good man, and also his son. But, Jennet, this still does not tell me what it is that troubles you, for I know in my heart there is something. Tom keeps asking about you and wonders what we have done to upset you, and even our dear friend, Roger . . ." (here Jennet stiffened perceptibly) "Roger keeps enquiring why it is you have never repeated your visit. He took quite a fancy to you, you know."

"I can hardly believe that is true," Jennet replied disdainfully, "but I assure you, Aunt, there is no fault on your part. It is just that I find myself unable to leave the farm."

Margaret looked closely at her niece. She had not missed the way in which Jennet had stiffened at the mention of Roger's name nor the scorn in her voice when she had spoken of him. So it was something to do with Roger! But what? She was sure they had never met before the day when they were both guests at her house. She sipped her wine, considering. She had to get to the bottom of this. She attacked without warning.

"Jennet, my dear," she said suddenly, "what is Roger Standerby to you?"

The look on Jennet's face told her here was the crux of the matter. She pressed on. "It is quite obvious to me that he is the reason why you have steadfastly refused to come to see us. Why, I cannot imagine, for he is a dear man. But I mean to find out, for I cannot and will not have this silly misunderstanding keeping us apart. If *you* will not tell me, then I must ask him."

"Then you will get no answer there, either," Jennet said in a strangled voice, "for he does not know. How could he when he has never seen me before that day I visited you?"

Margaret made a gesture of despair. "This mystery deepens by the minute. But I must know. I *will* know. Tell me, I beg of you, for the love we both bore your father!"

Jennet's face showed the strain she was, and had been, under. Then suddenly she crumpled, and broke into a storm of weeping. Margaret came across immediately, and took her in a warm motherly embrace. "Oh my poor child, my poor Jennet!" she murmured, almost in tears herself. "What is it? Tell your Aunt Meg, please!"

Then when Jennet was calmer, it all came out. She told her aunt, falteringly at first, but steadily growing stronger, about the raid on the farm, how old Jess, foolishly but bravely, tried to stop them, and died with his efforts. How they had hurt Jack, and taken away their goods and animals and damaged almost everything else. How she, with Mary, Sam and Jamie, had hidden in the store-cellar, and then had the barn fired over their heads.

"But you know all this, Aunt, for I wrote of it in my letters. But what I did not tell you was the name of the officer who so callously allowed his men to do this, nay, even ordered it, as I heard myself. It was Captain Standerby, as he was then. That name has haunted me since that day. I hate and despise him, and will do so until I die! I cannot bear to have him near me, and so when I found he was a privileged and frequent visitor to your house I felt it best to stay away, as well for your sake as mine, for I feared to cause you pain when you discovered what a monster he is. And now I have told you, and done the very thing I vowed not to do. Why did you make me do it?"

She began to weep again, a lost, lonely sort of weeping, like a child bereft of its parents and home. Margaret tried to comfort her, her own mind in turmoil. After a while, Margaret dried her own eyes, and offered a clean handkerchief to Jennet, whose weeping had died down to a few tearing sobs.

"Come, niece, dry your eyes and let us talk upon this matter. I must first tell you what I know about Roger. I cannot believe he is the man you think he is. It is not in his nature, and I have known him since I married my dear Tom. He was a lad of fifteen, I believe, when he lost his mother and father in a visitation of the plague in 1631. He and his elder brother and sister were visiting an aunt in Derbyshire at the time and so escaped the infection. They lived in a big, old house on the edge of the Yorkshire moors, and were not rich, for Roger's father had lost most of his money in a disastrous venture. So when the parents died, the house and whatever land there was, had to be sold to pay for their education and upkeep. The aunt, a straitlaced old lady, I have heard, became their guardian, and they lived with her until they were of an age to leave home. Roger's sister, of course, married early and went to live in London, I think that was her way of escape, for being a maid, she could not go out into the world unattended. However, the marriage turned out happily enough, for all its hasty arrangement, and she now has several children. Roger adores them for he has always loved children.

The boys stayed on for a while, under their aunt's strict rule, which they hated, as had their sister, but eventually the elder brother ran away and took service with a merchant who did a lot of overseas trade. He sailed with this merchant's ships, and is now a captain. Roger, left alone, had to bear with his aunt's increased malice, for she was incensed at his brother's departure and took out her displeasure on him. The only relief he had had was when he went away to school, and that was not much better for the masters there were strict disciplinarians. The school was, evidently, chosen by his aunt for this very purpose. But he was a studious, quiet boy and did well. My Tom has told me all this, for he had a nephew who was also at this school and Roger and he became friends. Through this, he became known to Thomas who had always been attached to his nephew.

Roger was invited to stay with his friend on several occasions.

The aunt, now in failing health, had been glad for him to be off her hands, during the boy's holidays. She died, at last, leaving him without a home and penniless, for perversely, she left everything to a distant relation."

Margaret paused, for breath it seemed, but really to see how Jennet was taking it. The girl sat entranced, interested in spite of herself, for she had determined at the outset not to be swayed by anything her aunt might say in mitigation of Master Roger Standerby.

Satisfied, Margaret went on.

"The lad was now almost nineteen, without anywhere to live. To his great joy, his friend John's parents, who were Thomas's sister and brother-in-law, saw great promise in the lad and invited him to live with them at their home in East Lancashire. Here, he was trained to manage John's father's estate and eventually became his steward.

Roger had now married John's cousin, a pretty, frail little creature, whom he adored, but alas, within a year she was dead, poor child, in childbirth, and the babe with her. Roger, I know was hard hit by this blow, and I wonder if he has yet recovered from it. During the war itself, Roger fought beside Tom and saved his life on more than one occasion." Margaret paused, her eyes sombre, as though she recalled some long ago event that caused her sadness. Then with an almost visible mental effort she resumed her tale.

"Yes, Roger was a reckless fighter and apt to rush in where others feared to go. It was as though he courted death, yet it passed him by. Tom has often told me how he thought this was so. He loves Roger like a son and so do I."

"But what had happened to his friend, John?" asked Jennet. "Did he not also join the King's forces?"

"Yes, but he was killed at Marston Moor. This, also, was a great sorrow to Roger for they were like brothers. Now he is again looking for a home for John's parents are dead too, within months of each other and their estate had been sequestrated by Parliament. We have often asked him to make his home with us, but he will have none of it, saying he wishes, at last, to have a home of his own. He has a small inheritance from his wife and has carefully saved it. He wants, he says, to buy a farm and manage it himself for his days managing John's father's estate have given him a love of the rural life. His earliest days were spent in the wild countryside of Yorkshire which he loved. Can you in all honesty, Jennet, having heard Roger's story, reconcile your own preconceived idea of him with this?"

Margaret sat back in her chair, her mouth dry from her long tale and took the glass which had stood unheeded on the table during all this. She sipped it, moistening her lips and mouth and gazing at her niece, trying to gauge her reaction.

Jennet sat bemused, her mind in conflict with her emotions. She stayed thinking for a moment. "Aunt Meg," she said at last, "I must, in fairness, say that the picture you have painted so vividly points to a man totally unlike the one I have held in revulsion since 1643. But I cannot help what I heard . Captain Standerby ordered his man, Fenton, I think his name was, to *question* Jack again. He also referred to him as an idiot . . . which he is not!" she added indignantly.

"You said 'question', Jennet. To my mind, that does not mean that Roger meant them to use Jack violently in order to force him to speak, however they chose to interpret it. And as you have yourself told me, Jack's former difficulty with speech made many people think he was lacking in wits."

"Yes, I know that, but he, Master Standerby, must have been there when it was done and when those men did all that damage and set fire so wantonly to the barn; he must have known and yet he did nothing to stop it. I could have forgiven them taking the food, for I know they were short of supplies. But how many folk have they left totally without food and starving? We were lucky that they did not find all we had, but they did not know that. As it was, that winter was the worst I have ever experienced, and I pitied with all my heart those poor folk who were in worse case than we were. Your precious Roger, who you say is so kind and loving, was, to a large extent, responsible, for he was the officer in charge of those men."

Margaret gazed at her with despair and yet with compassion. She had so hoped to change Jennet's mind, for she'd had something else in mind, (but no more of that for now) yet she could understand Jennet's point of view and what she thought had happened. She was rather puzzled herself. It certainly did not fit in with what she knew of Roger.

"Well, perhaps we should let it rest for the moment. But I should like to point out that these 'Clubmen', as Tom and Roger have told me, - and I suspect they were the ones who did you so much harm - were ill-disciplined and unruly and well-nigh uncontrollable, and only in the conflict for what plunder they could get. Now, let us consider ways and means by which we can re-continue our former loving relationship."

She smiled upon Jennet, who after a second, smiled back and then they were in each others arms, crying and laughing together.

So it was arranged that Margaret would visit her niece as often as she could, that Jennet would visit the Trenthams when it was known for certain that Roger Standerby would not be there. Margaret insisted she would have to tell Tom Jennet's reasons for not wanting to meet Roger, but gave in reluctantly to Jennet's insistence that Master Standerby should not be told anything. She secretly hoped that somehow Tom and herself could contrive some way in which the younger ones could come to know each other better. She felt sure that Jennet would begin to see Roger in a different light when she knew him as she, Margaret, knew him. But how to bring that about, without breaking her word to her niece, would be difficult. However, if one put one's mind to it, perhaps not impossible. . . .

CHAPTER FIFTEEN

They had been in there a long time, almost two hours. Mary was getting anxious. The carriage driver too, kept looking at the clock. Dickon had fallen asleep on the settle, tired at last of asking the driver innumerable questions. He had taken the little boy out to see the horse, still contentedly munching the hay Mary had given him, and had sat him on the horse's back and then in the driver's seat, and let him hold the whip. Dickon was delighted. He refused to come down, and had to be coaxed by the driver promising to take him for a ride, next time he came. He had fallen asleep in the man's arms eventually; and Mary put some blankets on the wooden settle and settled him there.

And still Mistress Jennet and her Aunt were in the parlour. What were they talking about? Mary had thought she heard the sound of someone weeping earlier on, but dare not go in to find out.

Then the sound of someone talking at length, the same voice all the time. It must have been Mistress Trentham, for it didn't sound like the young voice of Mistress Jennet's.

The driver began to fidget in his chair.

"Do ye think they will be much longer, Mistress?" he asked finally. "I know the lady is paying me for me time, but I would like to get home for me supper. Me wife gets fair annoyed if I be late, and 'tis getting on for four."

Mary hoped they would not be long, too. Their own supper was due at five and Jack and Sam and Jamie would be coming in soon from the field where they had started harvesting this year's crop of corn.

After a few more minutes, however, the parlour door opened and the two women came out. Mary was relieved to see that they were both smiling and looked very happy, although Mistress Jennet's eyes looked a bit red. The driver rose to his feet as the ladies came in.

"Oh Master Longhurst, I am sorry to have kept you waiting so long", said Margaret, "but we have had some very important business to discuss." She smiled at Jennet as she finished speaking.

Jennet said, "Has Mary kept you entertained, then, and given you something to eat?"

"Oh, yes Mistress, thank ye kindly," he replied, touching his forelock, "and the young Master, too. He be a bright 'un, that young 'un is, and no mistake." He thanked Mary too and went into the yard to turn the carriage round, Margaret said her farewells to Jennet, reminding her that she would see her the next week, said a few kind words to Mary, who curtsied her thanks, and looked at the sleeping Dickon, saying in a fond whisper, "Bless him, the little angel," and departed, waving to Jennet out of the carriage window.

Jennet came back into the kitchen, in an exuberant mood, and impulsively hugged Mary.

"Oh, Mary, my dear Mary! I am so glad. Aunt Meg and I are friends again and will be visiting each other. Well we were never really at odds, but there was something that kept us apart, and now dear Aunt Meg has found a way of solving it."

Mary said she too was glad to see her mistress so happy, but her mystified face made Jennet say, "Oh, I know you are wondering what it has all been about, and though I have never had any secrets from you before, there has been something I have never told you, which has been troubling me for a long time."

Mary admitted she had noticed something was amiss.

"You have? Then as today seems to be the day for confessions I will tell you what it is, but not yet, not until after supper at least, for here is Dickon waking up, and we have to get supper ready for those hungry men who will be here soon, declaring they are starving."

It was almost bed-time, however, before they had a chance to be alone. Jack declared after supper, that as there was still a couple of hours before dark, they must get back to their harvesting while they could, and took Sam and Jamie with him. Jennet was intending to tell Jack, too, because she felt that he was as much entitled to be in her confidence as Mary. They were as much a part of her life as the farm. Sam, she was not so sure about, she could not quite say why; Perhaps she was influenced by Jack's obvious dislike of the man. Jamie was a little young, and, in any case, she could not tell him without telling his father, too, even though they had both been involved in the events of which she was to speak.

Then when Jack had gone out with the others, Mary and she, after tidying the kitchen, had settled down to their sewing. She was going to tell Mary her secret over their mutual task. Dickon played in the yard for a short time before he had to go to bed. Jennet left the door open because it was a warm evening, and through it they could watch Dickon. They pulled their stools near the door to catch more light and also to feel the soft breeze blowing from the west. Through the gap between the shippon and the barn, they could see part of the long bluish line that was Longridge Fell.

Mary was impatiently waiting for Jennet to start. When she looked at her Mistress, she was gazing thoughtfully at the Fell, the sewing lying unheeded in her lap.

"Mistress Jennet . . ." she began, to bring Jennet back from wherever her thoughts had led her. Jennet was back in the past, reliving those events of early February in 1643. She had been there many times before, and now with a start, Mary's voice brought her back again.

"Oh, I am sorry, Mary," she said slowly, "I know you are agog to hear what I was going to tell you. Well - where shall I start? Oh yes - you remember when we were down in the cellar? When the Royalist soldiers came to the farm? Remember the man, the officer, whose voice. . . ."

She was interrupted by a shout from Dickon, and looked up, startled. Mary was on her feet, her sewing dropping to the floor. Jennet was behind as they reached the yard. They both thought Dickon was hurt, but he came running up, shouting, "Mammy! Mammy! Men on horses! Coming down the lane!"

For a second Jennet faltered, her heart missed a beat. Her thoughts had been, just a moment before, at the scene of which she had started to speak to Mary, she had seen, in her mind's eye, the soldiers advancing on the farm, the officer on his horse, directing operations. True, she had never actually seen them, but they were there as she had imagined them. And now, almost as though thoughts had become reality, as though the images in her mind had, by some magic, taken solid shape, there they were coming into the yard. Not the mob of clubmen, nor even orderly soldiers, nor were they armed, either with pikes, clubs, swords or muskets. Just two men, one on horseback, with clothes and hair which proclaimed him a gentleman, the other, more roughly dressed and with a limp, holding on the the horse's bridle.

She knew them both. The man on foot was Harry Baines, the horserider, Roger Standerby. The latter alighted, swept off his hat and bowed, and advanced, holding out his hand to take hers. Harry stood still holding the horse, his left hand on the bridle, his right uplifted to his forehead in a clumsy salute.

Jennet was rooted to the spot. Standerby took her hand and raised it to his lips. Again that queer feeling assailed her. She felt weak at the knees, and hoped she was not going to make a fool of herself by fainting.

He was speaking now in that cultured voice she remembered so well.

"My deepest apologies, Mistress, for intruding on you so impolitely, but I was in the district after looking at the farm I am interested in, and knew from your previous visit to Mistress Trentham's, your aunt's, that you lived near by, but not exactly where. I desired, therefore, to renew our acquaintance. Forgive me if I was being importunate - then by the greatest good fortune, I came to this young man, Master Baines, I believe, who informed me he was coming here, and would direct me. I trust I am not inconveniencing you?" He bowed again and looked at her anxiously.

A thousand things flashed through Jennet's mind in an instant. he could not say he didn't know where this farm was when he had been here before. True, he did not know this was her farm. Well, he did now, but had not shown it by so much as the flicker of an eyelash. And how had he known that Whitegate Farm was now vacant? Had Aunt Meg told him? No, that could not be for she did not know herself until Jennet told her indirectly this afternoon, and how was she so certain it was Whitegate Farm? He had not said so.

The instant passed and then she found herself murmuring something bidding him come inside for a drink, after his long ride. She must keep up appearances, especially with the man, Harry Baines, standing there, although her first instinct had been to scream out loud and beg Roger Standerby to go away, out of her life, to leave her alone, for hadn't he done enough to her already?

Instead, she forced herself to remain calm, was polite, but distant, and preceded him into the house, where she directed the round-eyed Mary to show him into the parlour and provide him with a drink of ale or wine whichever he should prefer.

He stopped her politely, however, and said with a diffident smile (how unlike him, she thought) that he would not dream of troubling her so much, that the kitchen would do very well and as for a drink, yes, he was thirsty he must admit, and a cup of ale would quench it more than wine, if she did not mind. Oh, and he must not forget Master Baines, whose business with her was prior to his. The young man, from what he said, was anxious to see her.

Jennet therefore, excused herself and curtsied, and went out to where Harry was waiting anxiously with the horse.

"You wanted to see me, Harry?" she asked, "I did not know you were back from the war. I have not heard of you since you left. I was sorry to hear of your mother's death and I believe your sister has gone into service in Preston."

"Aye, Mistress, and I did not know of it meself until I come back, but yestere'en. The cottage is let to another family, too."

"So now you have nowhere to live? What a pity!"

"That's reet, Mistress, and I were wondering, seeing as how your farm animals have increased, so I've heard, if you would be needing another hand now."

She paused, considering. Jack had mentioned how they could do with another hand, for the time being, at any rate while they were harvesting.

"Well, Harry, I can't promise you a permanent job, we will see about that later, perhaps. But Jack is needing another hand for the harvest at present. He is there now in the long meadow with Sam and Jamie, so go up there and say I sent you. He will be glad to see you, I am sure. Tie that horse up somewhere, see Jack, and then come back here for something to eat. I'm sure you are hungry." Harry thanked her, tied up the horse and then made to run off to the long meadow. She noticed his limp then, and called him back.

"Harry, are your sure you can manage the work? I see you have hurt your leg. Are you alright?"

"Oh that! Mistress, that's nowt, I got a pike thrust at Naseby, but 'tis all better now. Has been for a long time. It won't stop me none, see, Mistress!"

And to prove it he started running towards the field where Jack and the others were. After about fifteen yards he stopped, turned round, jumped into the air, then saluted her with a cheeky grin and set off again.

Jennet turned back to the house, still smiling at his antics, then, remembering who was there waiting for her, became grave again. She didn't want to go back and face him, but it had to be done, so smoothing her dress and setting her cap to rights she gave herself a mental shake and went in.

He was sitting at the table with his back to her, chatting quite amicably to Mary, who seemed to have got over her initial shock at entertaining this fine gentleman, but more particularly with the irrepressible Dickon, who, with his usual forthrightness was asking questions of the stranger. She had come in quietly, so they had not noticed her. She stood for a few seconds watching. He was dressed in a maroon velvet coat with the usual wide lace collar. His breeches, from what she could see from under the table, were a dark green, she thought. His light cloak, thrown over the back of the settle, was the same colour and his hat was black with a curling feather round the brim, now on the table where Dickon was playing with it.

Dickon was saying, "What sort of bird is this from, Sir? It must be a big one."

"Yes, Dickon, it is. It is the largest bird in the world."

"What's it called, then?"

"An Ostrich, my lad."

"A Nostwich? I never heard of one of those. Are there any round here?"

"No Dickon, they come from a land a long way from here, where it is always hot."

"Always? Don't they have any winter, then, with snow and ice?"

By now, Jennet decided the conversation had gone on long enough. Knowing Dickon, it could last all night. So she made a show of closing the door more noisily, and they all looked round.

Quickly, Roger sprang to his feet, in deference to her entrance. He certainly had perfect manners, she reflected wryly.

"Dickon, it is past eight o'clock and long past your bed-time. Come along now, and cease pestering Master Standerby."

The child set up a wail which was quickly stopped by a look from his mother. Roger took up his hat and cloak and said he must leave. He had no idea it was so late, he had been so entertained by young Dickon and Mistress Mary. He apologised for coming so late in the day. It was unforgivable of him, but he fervently hoped she would find it in her heart to do so. Perhaps, when and if he decided to buy the vacant farm, she would do him the honour of dining with him. In the meantime, might he be allowed to call on her, some time, earlier in the day, of course?

Hardly knowing what to say, Jennet made the usual non-committal answer of being very busy, but, strangely enough, couldn't bring herself to say 'no' outright, finally and irrevocably. She raged at herself after he had gone, calling herself a weak-kneed fool, without the courage of her convictions, and every other thing she could think of.

But always came back the memory of him sitting there so patiently answering Dickon's questions, and the child's face, looking so trustingly up into his. They said children always knew. And then with another change of mood, she thought, but Dickon is like that with everyone, so it doesn't prove anything.

CHAPTER SIXTEEN

By the time they had got Dickon settled, Harry was back, and they prepared a meal for him. He had not eaten all day, he said, and fell on the meal with gusto.

"Master Jack were glad to see me," he told them, his mouth full. "My, I hardly recognised him, he's grown such a big 'un, and he don't talk so funny any more. He's like a different chap. He said they'll be back shortly as it's getting too dark to see, and I'll be starting work wi 'em in t'morning. That Sam don't say much, but Jamie be a likely lad. I were surprised to see 'em still 'ere, some'ow I never thowt they'd stick it, at least, not Sam."

"Why do you say that? Sam has been quite a good worker and he seems settled enough".

"Oh, I dunno, Mistress, it's just a feeling I had. Well, I be glad he turned out all reet." He smiled at them both, but his eyes lingered on Mary, Jennet noticed. She remembered something.

"Oh, by the way, weren't you going to marry Alison Starkie? What happened? Have you seen her?"

He looked a bit rueful, "Aye, Mistress, I seen her yesterday. She got tired o' waiting and married the blacksmith. She has a little 'un and another on't way. But I can't blame her, she never knew when I were coming back."

Jennet remembered then that Mary had told her of it, but she had forgotten in the welter of events that had happened since then, and her own preoccupation with them. She had also forgotten how she had determined to do something about Mary's secret hankering after Jack. But looking at the way Harry was eyeing the girl, and Mary's own blushes under his scrutiny, perhaps events might be allowed to take their own course. What could she have done, anyway?

If Jack was not really interested, perhaps it would be as well if Mary did turn her attention to someone else. In other words, to

Harry. So she could just let things happen as they would. In the meantime, she had other worries on her mind. Such as, what was she going to do about Roger Standerby? If he did come to live at Whitegate Farm, they would be neighbours, and she did not think she could bear to live with him so near at hand and perhaps calling on her frequently, which he seemed determined to do. There was also the question of what she was to tell Mary now. Somehow, his visit seemed to put a different complexion on it. She didn't know why but now she was reluctant to tell the girl, or Jack either, of her feelings.

But then the others came in, tired and thirsty, demanding food and drink after their labours. The talk turned to matters relating to the farm, and then Harry began to tell them of his adventures in the war, egged on by Jamie. He kept them enthralled for hours. It was late when they all went to bed, too tired for anything but to fall on their various places of rest and sink immediately into exhausted sleep.

On Wednesday of the next week, Aunt Meg came as promised, and Jennet was kept occupied showing her around the farm. Of course, she knew it well, having lived there until her first marriage, but she declared it was all so changed and improved she did not recognise it. She congratulated Jennet on her expert management.

"Well, Jack takes charge of the farm work now, Aunt, I leave it all to him, and he has become very knowledgeable. I do not know what I would do without him, and this is the lad some people used to call an idiot." She cast a meaningful glance at Meg, who smiled ruefully.

"Oh, I know to whom you are referring, Jennet, in particular, but he was not the only one, as you will know, Jack must be one of those whom Tom calls 'late in developing' - though there is no doubt that having only just met him, I can hardly believe he is the same person you told me was once called 'Simple Jack'. And that reminds me. . . ."

She began to speak of that which she had obviously been dying to mention since her arrival. Jennet knew he would have told her aunt of his visit to her.

"Roger tells me he called on you last week. I am sure you were surprised to see him. He says he heard of your neighbour's farm being put up for sale, and came to look at it. Knowing you lived in the neighbourhood, he decided to pay his respects. It was wrong of him to call so late in the evening, as he readily admitted, and hoped you would not think ill of him, He was very much taken with Dickon, and has spoken of him many times."

She kept looking narrowly at Jennet, while trying to appear not to do so, but the girl, knowing what was coming, kept her feelings rigidly under control, and showed no reaction. Meg ploughed relentlessly on.

"I think he has decided finally to buy the farm, so you will be neighbours and will not be able to avoid meeting each other. What say you, Jennet? Do you think you will be able to come to terms with him and forget the past?"

This time she looked pointedly anxious. She had been meaning to tell Roger of the vacant farm, persuade him to buy it and so force the two into meeting. This way, she could have kept her word to Jennet, devious though it was. She had been overjoyed when she found that Roger had forestalled her, by finding out about the farm himself and in coming to call on Jennet. It seemed as though Providence was stepping in , to bring her plans to fruition. That is, if Jennet could be persuaded to accept him as a friend. Jennet's reply was not hopeful.

"I do not think that will be likely, Aunt. My father and I lived for years without coming into contact much with the Towneleys. We were virtual strangers to each other until my father became ill and Jack ran to them for help, because I was not there. I was glad in a way, eventually, apart from their help during Father's illness and death, because it brought me my dear Richard, who I had for so short a time. No other man could be to me what he was, and I thank God constantly that I have my little Dickon, who is so like him."

There, that was it, she had implied to Aunt Meg to keep off, that there was no chance of it happening; the thing that she sensed, rather than positively knew, was in her Aunt's mind. But Meg, of course, was made of sterner stuff; she, too, had the Gregson blood in her veins, and like John, Jennet's father, and Jennet herself, could be very obstinate.

She took her leave, saying no more on the subject, but biding her time. She did, however, extract a promise from Jennet, to come on the next market day, but one, to visit Tom and her in Preston.

"For it is now October, my dear, and winter draws on apace, it may be the last time we can meet if the winter should prove to be a hard one. You know what the roads and lanes can be like. Nothing can get through. I would have liked for you to see us over Christmas, but would not ask you to come through the bad weather and besides, I know you will want to spend Christmas here. While the weather holds, of course, we will still meet."

"Will - will he be there?"

"Who? Tom?" replied Margaret airily, being deliberately obtuse.

"Of course he will be there. You wish to see him, do you not? Or have you taken a dislike to him, too?"

Jennet laughed in spite of herself. "Aunt Meg, you know who I mean."

"Oh, Roger! No, he will not. He has some business to attend to in Clitheroe, something to do with the inheritance he received from his late wife. He will be away all that weekend, I believe. Well, I must go, I have kept you long enough away from your dairy. Give my love to Dickon and my regards to the others."

Dickon was with Mary and the men in the cornfield. Mary had taken to spending as much time as she could spare out there, but always took Dickon with her, saying it would do him good to be out in the fresh air and sunshine.

Jennet could not argue with that, but reflected that the boy got plenty of that, anyway. He was invariably outside, playing in the yard or in the garden. But Jennet knew perfectly well the real reason for Mary's wanting to be with the men. Well, good fortune to her!

The weather did not deteriorate until well into November, although it was cold, the skies remained clear, so Jennet and her aunt were able to exchange a few more visits. Uncle Tom was sympathetic, but his advice, when he took her aside once, was uncompromising.

"Bring it all out into the open! All this playing hide and seek is childish, my dear. You must meet Roger some time, now that he is to live next door to you. Do, next time you see him, tell him everything. Tell him that you know he is the officer who was there when your farm was raided. Give him a chance to explain."

"Explain!" she cried, "What is there to explain? Nothing can justify his callous conduct."

"All I can say is, as Meg has told me, you refuse utterly to consider if there were any mitigating circumstances. You are condemning poor Roger out of hand, without hearing his side. How do you know he was even there? I mean, after you heard him speak can you say for sure he was still there when the clubmen did the damage? I knew these men and what they were capable of, and I know Roger, and nothing will convince me he condoned this. I wish you would let your aunt or me speak to him and find out the truth. Or why don't you do it yourself?"

But Jennet still refused to give in, and begged Uncle Tom not to say anything. He agreed reluctantly, but made her, in turn, promise to think it over in the light he had presented it to her.

So, true to her word she did, and had to admit, that after she had heard Roger's voice, she had fainted, and heard nothing more. But there were other people who were there, Mary, Sam and the boy. And Jack, who must have seen more than any of them. She had never questioned him closely as to what had occurred, not wanting to disturb him further by reminding him of that traumatic experience. Nor had she wished to speak of it for her own sake, it was too awful to recall.

Now she must. She had never told Mary nor Jack as she had said she would. Jack knew nothing of it, of course, but Mary had often looked at her reproachfully and started to speak, then thought better of it. Now she seemed to have forgotten all about it, immersed as she was in flirting with Harry.

Harry, of course, was still with them, though the harvesting was long over. He had begged to be allowed to stay until the new owner came to take over Whitegate Farm, for everyone knew that it had been sold. There was always the chance, he said, of finding permanent work there for they would be sure to want hands come January, for the ploughing. Jennet was not averse to this for she was a kind-hearted girl, and Harry did make himself useful.

The kitchen, large though it was, was becoming crowded at meal-times and when they were all gathered together in the evenings. So it was a relief to have the parlour, to which she could retire. The extension to the house had stretched to the parlour downstairs, and two small rooms above. Jack now slept in one of these and Sam in the other, while Jamie used Jack's old box bed in the kitchen. So they were now all housed inside, and could retire to their own rooms for privacy if they wished. All except Jamie, whose bed was in the kitchen. Harry was sleeping in the barn.

None of them, however, seemed to feel the need to be by themselves, and since the arrival of Harry Baines, their evenings were entertaining. He had a fund of stories to tell, tricks with which to mystify, and he enlivened their evenings greatly.

Jennet wished to get Mary and Jack on their own, but it was difficult. Finally, one afternoon in mid December, when Mary and she were preparing the plum cakes and other goodies for Christmas, and the men were in the barn about their winter tasks of sending and overhauling equipment, she felt the time to be right. It had started to snow the day before and it was still falling. If it kept on like this they would be snowed in by Christmas. They were well stocked up and had plenty of peat, logs and firewood, brought last summer from the moor, and allowed to dry out. Some time, when she was better off, Jennet thought she would like to try some sea-coal, which her aunt had told her of, but it was very expensive.

Now the cakes were in the oven, or baked and cooling on the table, ready to be packed away for when they were needed.

So she sent Mary out to the barn, shawled and well shod, to ask Jack to come to her on some business regarding the farm.

They came in together, shaking the snow from their clothes and exchanging their outdoor footwear for lighter shoes, which Jennet insisted upon. She led them into the parlour where a fire was lit, making the room cosy and warm. She wanted them to be private, if they stayed in the kitchen one of the others might come in for something or other.

She bade them be seated; Jack however, would not sit on her elegant chairs in his rough work clothes, and went to fetch a stool from the kitchen.

"I have something to tell you," she began, "and I have to ask you something. Something which means a lot to me."

She paused. Supposing they did not remember, or had not seen or heard anything. But she must keep on, she had to know, one way or the other.

So she started right from the beginning, took them both back to the day when the Royalists had come, told them who the officer was and her own connection with him, and how she had brooded upon it all the time, unable to believe that Roger Standerby was other than a cold-blooded, callous man, worthy only to be hated and despised by decent folk.

"Now I must ask you both what you saw or heard during that dreadful day. I want to know if that man, Captain Standerby, as he was then, was a party to it all. Did he, in truth, order it?"

Mary spoke first, and surprisingly.

"Well, Mistress, I knew who he was, that day he came here to see you. I remembered his name, too, but not at first, it came to me after. I thought he was a very nice gentleman and he was so good with Dickon. As for that day you speak of, I did not hear him any more after that first time he spoke, I don't think so, anyway, 'tis such a long time ago, 'tis so hard to remember." She thought hard, obviously trying to jog her memory. Then she brightened, "There was the sound of a horse, going out of the farmyard, and seemed to be some men marching. This was just after the Captain had been in the barn. But there was still more noise came afterwards like shouting, and a lot of crashing and banging. Then they must have set the barn on fire. I tell you, Mistress Jennet, I thought me last day had come, I was that frightened. We could hear the flames and the smoke started to come into the cellar. We were all coughing and choking. It was a relief to see Master Towneley's face when he opened the trap door, though I confess I thought it was those men come back when he and his man were moving the wood to get it open."

"Thank you, Mary," said Jennet, "now just go and see if those cakes are alright in the oven; you can come back if you wish to hear what Jack has to say. And you, Jack, please try to remember as much as you can, I know it was a terrible time for you, but it is important."

Jack had been sitting hunched on his stool while Mary told her story. He said nothing until Mary came back and settled herself in her chair. He was staring into the fire, perhaps seeing there scenes for which he was searching in his memory.

Jennet prompted him gently, "Well, Jack, what do you remember?"

He looked round almost dazedly, his gentle, blue eyes not seeing her. They found Mary's and she smiled encouragingly, and groped for his hand, edging her chair neared to his.

"Come on Lad" she urged him, "tell the Mistress what happened. 'Tis only you can set her mind at rest, I'm thinking."

He began, slowly at first, trying to recollect, and put into order the memories that came crowding. Then his voice came strong and clear.

"'Tis not all clear, Mistress, I have not thought of it for years, it may be that I did not wish to think of it. I remember when Jess tried to stop them and fell, I went to run to him, but they pulled me away. I kept thinking of the poor old man, lying there on the cold ground. There was no officer with them, then, he must have gone round by the lane, while they had come over the fields.

When they dragged me into the yard, he was there, just getting off his horse. There were some proper soldiers with him, with armour and muskets and some had pikes. They were very orderly, but the men who came over the fields and dragged me away from Jess were a rough lot, armed only with sticks and staves, and some with pitchforks and other farm tools. They took me over to the officer, this Captain Standerby, you say. He asked where the farmer was and if we had any food. I couldn't answer, I was so afraid. I tried to say we had nothing, but couldn't get out the words. I wondered where you all were, Mistress, and hoped you had managed to hide. Then the Captain went over to the barn with one of the soldiers, the sergeant he must have been. They came out after a while, I thought they must have been checking if the men who had been searching it had missed anything. I thought of the cellar, and if you had somehow hidden in there, and was glad they had not found it.

Then the Captain said to take what they could find in the way of food as the tenants or owners appeared to have got away with most of it, but to leave everything else. He got on to his horse then, telling the sergeant to see if they could get anything more out of the 'idiot'. I reckon he meant me." He gave a grim chuckle, then went on. "He said he was going on to the next farm, to see what could be got there, with some of the wagons and animals and about half his men, including most of the soldiers. The others were to go back to their headquarters with what they had got. Then they all went off towards Master Towneley's. The other men, left behind, instead of going on as they had been ordered, waited a few minutes until the captain and the others had gone and then they started to carry on like a pack of devils.

I didn't see much of what they did. This man who had been told to question me started knocking me about and kicking me, shouting to tell them where our food and money were. I was on the floor trying to protect my head with my arms, but he kept hitting me with a stick. Then all I remember is someone coming up to stop him and saying they must go in case the captain came back, or they'd catch it for not obeying orders. After that, I must have lost me senses for I knew nothing more."

He looked at Jennet then, questioning, "Is that what you wanted to know, Mistress? Does it help?"

Jennet looked pensive for a moment, going over it in her mind. Then,

"Yes, Jack, it does," she said, "it tells me that Captain Standerby was not wholly responsible and that is what I wanted to know. But tell me, what did you think of him? Did he strike you as cold-hearted, vicious man, as I have thought of him all these years?"

"Lord, no, Mistress! Begging your pardon, I thought he was just doing as he'd been ordered, and not liking it much, either. It was plain he didn't think much of those others, those 'clubmen', you called them? Looking back now, I can see him quite plain. A lonely sort of man, he seemed, with a kind of sadness about his face. It seemed to me he were miles away. Well, that's what *I* thought anyway. I could have been wrong."

Jennet's eyes were shining. She said in a low, wondering voice. "No, Jack, I do not think you were." Then with a new decisiveness, "Now, my dear friends let us get back to our work. You have helped me more than you know. I shall never forget it."

She rose, and they did, too. Mary, as though coming to herself, hurriedly detached her hand from Jack's, with a blush spreading over her face. Jack sought to take it again, but she eluded him, slipping out of the door, into the kitchen. Jennet, despite the inner turmoil of her own thoughts, noticed this little by-play and smiled to herself. It seemed as though their shared reminiscences had drawn them together as nothing else could.

CHAPTER SEVENTEEN

Now that she had resolved, as far as was possible in the circumstances, the doubts, uncertainties, even prejudices, she had sustained for so long, Jennet should have been happier in her mind. That she was not, was due to some extent to the continued absence of Roger Standerby. He had never returned to pay the call he had promised to make, and she had not been able to see her aunt since the bad weather had descended on them. He had not been there, of course, on her last few visits - her aunt and uncle had been true to their promise - and she herself had not then questioned Jack and Mary.

Now she wanted above all else to see him again, not, she assured herself, for any sentimental reasons, but to clear any last lingering doubts. She must do this, in fairness to Aunt Meg and Uncle Tom, if not to herself. She wanted to study his face, which she had never really done before. Always she had kept her glance averted, because she had felt she could not bear to look at him straightly. She wanted to hear from his own lips what had been in his mind that day, how he had felt.

She knew he had not been back to Whitegate Farm, but there had been men working at the farmhouse before the weather closed down, and much coming and going. One of them, who said he was a carpenter, had come to Gregson's Farm to buy some produce. He told her he did not know when the new owner was coming to live there, only that he and some others had been sent there to make some alterations, and to paint and re-furbish the interior of the house.

Now for weeks there had been no sign of life. It was Christmas Eve. Snow lay deep on the fields, in drifts against the walls and hedges. They had cleared the yard, piling up the snow against the buildings, and a narrow path up the lane to their gate. It was hardly worth it, for there was no going beyond it, but it gave the men something to do and kept them warm, doing all that hard work. It also made them hungry. Jennet and Mary were kept hard at work making meals and keeping Dickon occupied and happy, and decorating the house with holly and mistletoe. In the afternoon they were in the yard helping Dickon build a snowman, and soon were in the thick of a snowfight, started by Jamie hurling a handful of snow at Harry, who retaliated. Then Mary joined in, and it wasn't long before they were all at it, except Sam, who felt it beneath his dignity to behave so childishly. He clumped back inside to warm his numbed hands before the fire.

Outside, they were still enjoying themselves, Jennet as much as anyone. She stooped down, gathered a handful of snow from the pile against the barn and threw it with all her force at Jack, who ducked. The snow ball sailed over his head straight at the figure of a man who had halted, unnoticed, between the shippon and the dairy where the lane leading to the farm gate began. He had been quietly watching them for minutes, and then suddenly was hit in the face by the snowball.

Jennet's hands flew to her face in horror. Then the man, after his initial shock, laughed aloud. He advanced, taking off his hat, and bowed.

Jennet, her heart beating thunderously, gasped, "Master Standerby! I - I am sorry, sir, I did not see you standing there."

"I know you did not, Mistress," he replied, smiling. "It was my own fault for standing in the line of fire, as it were, and partly this young man's" - indicating Jack, standing sheepishly by - "for so adroitly evading your well-aimed shot. But don't let me interrupt the game. It was a pleasure to watch you all enjoying yourselves so much. 'Tis many years since I, too, hurled snowballs at my friends."

"Then play with us!" shouted Dickon, preparing to scoop up another handful of snow.

"No, Dickon, no!" - his mother hastened to stop him, "Master Standerby, how have you come here, through the snow? And I - we thought you were not coming to live at Whitegate Farm yet, at least not until the spring."

"Mistress Towneley, I have been at Whitegate Farm since just after the snow started. I could not wait until the spring to be in my own home. The workmen have not finished their work yet, 'tis true, but I manage well enough in the two rooms which are reasonably well advanced in renovation."

"You are living there, and alone, Sir?" asked Jennet incredulously, "but what about furniture, and a bed? I do not think Master Towneley left anything there" - remembering guiltily that she possessed all of William and Alice's surplus furniture.

"Mistress," he interposed quickly, "I will answer all of your questions and more, but do you think you could wait until we are inside? It is a trifle c'cold out here, with your permission, of c'course."

Jennet realised suddenly that he was shivering, and his teeth were beginning to chatter. She saw, too, that his clothes were wet from the waist down.

"Oh, Master Standerby! and to think I have kept you standing out here in the cold. You are wet through, too. Come inside quickly please."

When she had hurried him inside, and ousted a grumbling Sam from where he was toasting himself on the settle before the fire, she made Master Standerby sit there and get warm.

"But you cannot stay in those wet clothes. Now what shall we do?" She thought for a moment. "Ah yes, the very thing!"

She sent Jack into the parlour to get some clothes from the teak chest. William had left them in there when he gave her the furniture, saying they had been his father's and he had no use for them, but perhaps they would come in useful for one or other of her farmhands. They were much too small for Jack and she had made over some breeches and jackets for Sam, but there were one or two other items of clothing which she had kept, in case they should be needed. They were needed now. How glad she was she had kept them. Only last week she had been thinking of sending them down to the village for some of the needy folk there.

Jack came back with an armful of clothes. She picked out a pair of breeches, a woollen shirt and jerkin, some thick woollen stockings.

"Here you are," she said thrusting them at Roger, "they are not what you have been used to, I am afraid, but they are clean and dry and you must change into them right away. Jack will take you up to his chamber to change. Oh, and Mary, take up some hot water for Master Standerby to wash. Harry, you can make up the fire in the parlour."

Like a little general she was, directing her troops, thought Roger Standerby, following Jack up the stairs. She was completely at her ease, now that she was in command of the situation, and able to do something that was going to help someone, not like on those other few occasions when they had met, when she seemed so ill at ease and distant in her manner.

He recalled how he had referred to her to the Trenthams, as 'the shy, cold little Puritan'. Then he remembered how she had looked just now in the yard, before she had seen him. She was laughing delightedly, her cheeks flushed, and her eyes sparkling, playing in the snow like a child, and the others like children with her. They were like friends together, not like mistress and servants. He wished that he could join their company. He could never think of her now as 'the shy, cold, little Puritan'. Not now, nor ever again.

When he re-appeared a little while later, Jennet could not suppress a smile, he looked so comical, so much a figure of fun in his incongruous clothes. The breeches were a trifle short, and large round the waist, which he had tried to remedy by buckling his belt tightly round it. The shirt and jerkin were obviously meant for a more corpulent man - dear old stout Will! - and the shirt sleeves much too long. He had had to turn them up several times. As for the stockings! Will had obviously had much larger feet. He had no shoes. His own boots were wet through inside and out, and there were no others in the house to fit him. He was a tall man, though nowhere as tall as Jack, and of a slender build.

He came in, grinning with embarrassment, obviously aware of what he looked like, but determined to carry it off with aplomb. He pirouetted around for their inspection, the effect of which was spoilt by his tripping over the long toes of his stockings which were sticking out inches from his own smaller feet. Everyone laughed, but not unkindly, and he seemed to sense this. He became, at once, more at ease.

Jennet said, "Come, Master Standerby, Mary has made some nourishing broth, which you must surely need, and we are about to take some for our supper. Will you have yours in the parlour? The fire is lit in there and it will be warm."

"By no means, Mistress, by your leave. If I am to be a farmer then I must begin to act like one, and have my meals in the kitchen, and as for your amusement over my clothes - and I am happy indeed to have been the means of making you laugh - then you must get used to the sight of me wearing such serviceable homespun dress, for I mean to wear such in my new role, although I confess" - he made a rueful face - "I shall see that I get a better fit next time."

Again the good-natured laughter, in which he joined most heartily. Then Jennet summoned everyone to the table. It was a tight squeeze, and there were not enough chairs or stools to go round in the kitchen, so others had to be brought in from the other rooms.

When they had finished the mutton broth, and had gooseberry tart made from Jennet's preserves, and for those who were still hungry, bread and cheese, they sat talking over their mulled ale.

Roger looked warm and relaxed, although he had sneezed once or twice - she hoped he had not caught cold - and was gazing round contentedly, at their warm, friendly, country faces.

They had accepted him; he could feel it, and was happy.

Jennet asked, "Now, Sir, will you not tell us how you came to be here? I am curious as to how you have spent nearly two weeks in that empty house. It is strange that we did not notice anyone was there, although now I come to think of it no one has been in the fields for some time, and one can only see the house at Whitegate Farm from our own long meadow."

Clearing his throat and taking a long drink of his ale, Master Standerby began to explain.

"But first," he said, smiling round on them all, "I must thank you for your hospitality, and your most kind welcome to one who is almost a stranger, or was, may I now say? To you, Mistress Jennet, and to you, Mistress Mary," - raising his cup to each, - "my compliments on a most excellent meal. I do not think I have enjoyed a better." He drank, and then continued.

"Now to my tale. When I first came to look around the farm next door I was much taken with it. It needed some minor repairs and some painting, but it was just what I had been looking for. Up in one of the attics I had noticed a camp-bed and an old table and stools, so when my longing to be in my own home grew too much for me I rode up here. I had ordered my furniture to arrive in January, but I felt I could manage until then. There was wood in one of the out-houses so I could make a fire and I had brought some food, but unfortunately not enough. After the first day, I had intended to call on you to pay my respects, and to buy some produce from you, if you could spare it. But when I woke up in the morning the snow was deep. I decided to wait until the next day or even the next, to see if the weather should improve.

It didn't, as you know, so I was faced with the dilemma of staying there and starving to death, or trying to dig myself out. There was only one solution, to my mind. I found an old spade in the barn and started to dig a path. It was not easy, I assure you. Many times I wanted to give up and go back to the warmth of my fire and sleep, even if I had very little food left, and would starve very soon.

But I kept on, sustained let me tell you by the thought of this farm, and of the warmth and food I hoped to find here, which I must admit was not as great as I have actually found here tonight. Your welcome and hospitality have far exceeded my expectations.

It took me nearly a week, and when I got to the lane, which

was only discernible by the hedges on either side, and then not always, it was much harder and I kept falling into drifts and once into a frozen pond, which fortunately was not deep, when I had missed the lane and gone over into a field. I managed to find the lane again and great was my joy when I saw the buildings of your farm and then the path which you had already dug. I cast my spade aside and came down the path to find you all besporting yourselves in the snow. You cannot imagine my relief, and, may I add, my amazement to find you all actually *enjoying* playing with snow! I never want to touch the stuff again!"

He grimaced with mock distaste and shuddered delicately, and then shivered again and gave a monumental sneeze. "Your pardon, my friends, I must have caught a chill. Atishoo!"

Jennet hurriedly brought a shawl and put it round his shoulders.

"Master Standerby, I fear you *have* caught cold. There is no question of your going back to that cold, empty house tonight. You must stay here."

"But Mistress, I could not put you to so much trouble, you have already done so much. I will be alright, I assure you. And there is my horse. I must get back to -"

"I will not hear of it, Sir. You *shall* stay here. As for your horse, Jack and Harry will get it for you. It should not be too difficult now you have, as you say, cleared a path through to Whitegate Farm. They can also bring your camp-bed and you can sleep in the parlour. Harry is sleeping here in the kitchen at the moment, now the weather is so cold. Oh, and by the way, Harry has something to ask you, but it will do when he returns. You do not mind going, do you?" She turned to the men in enquiry.

They signified their willingness to go, Harry flashing her a look of gratitude for paving the way with Master Standerby about the job he was hoping for. Jamie asked to go, too. He could hold the lantern, he said, for it was now dark.

They went, taking more shovels, in case they should need to widen the path, Jamie leading the way and obviously treating it as a great lark. Dickon wanted to go, too, but was refused firmly by his mother. He was too young, she said, to be out after dark.

"I'm four," he protested indignantly, "and I will soon be five. In February," he confided to Master Standerby.

"Oh, really!" remarked that gentleman earnestly. "You are really that old? And in February, eh? I must remember that."

Dickon looked eagerly at him and was about to say something but thought better of it. Mammy said he must not ask things like that. Instead he said, "But it is Mammy's birthday before mine. Hers is in January, the 4th or 5th, I think. Which is it, Mam?"

But "Mam" was having no more of this conversation and bade her son cease his prattling and help Mary get some blankets out for Master Standerby's bed, and then - at which he pulled a face - he could help her with the dishes, before it was his bed-time.

CHAPTER EIGHTEEN

The next morning, Christmas Day, dawned bright and clear and there was hope that the weather would improve. The sky, a pale, washed-out blue, was comparatively free of clouds, and a watery sun shone down coldly. There was a fresh breeze blowing, stirring the branches of the trees and making little falls of powdery snow.

Jennet stood in the yard, her shawl close about her face, admiring the scene. It was beautiful, the snow covering up the imperfections, making fairy patterns on the trees, even disguising the dungheap in the corner. Only where they had dug through the snow and dirtied it with their footprints was it spoiled.

But she was looking beyond that. The fields were unsullied, and the line of Longridge Fell was nearly indiscernible where a faint mist curled about its slopes. Yes, it was beautiful, and deadly.

Supposing he had fallen into a deep drift and been unable to get out? He would have lain there and frozen to death, and not been found until the snow melted. Or, supposing he had stayed in that empty house without food, and eventually without a fire, for he had said the wood was also getting low? But why was she standing here thinking these gloomy thoughts when he was here, safe and warm in her house? Contrarily, she wanted the snow to continue cutting them off from the world, and then he would have to remain.

She was only now beginning to realise why she had had him so much in her thoughts, since that day when she had bumped into him when she was leaving her aunt's house. She knew now that it was guilt that had clouded her reasoning. Guilt, because she was attracted secretly to a man who, she thought, was the epitome of all that was hateful, and was, as well, a member of that enemy force that had killed Richard, and was indirectly the cause of Jess's death, and who had caused so much hurt to Jack. She had been confused and remorseful, but now she knew the truth, or most of it. She thought too, she was beginning to know the man, and longed to know more.

She wished they could be alone and yet she shrank from it. But in that house it was virtually impossible, unless she pointedly invited him into the parlour, or rather, now he was sleeping there, herself to go in there when he was alone. It was not possible, not 'seemly'. She smiled sadly, thinking of her father.

Well, she had wasted enough time out here, there was so much to do today. Christmas dinner to prepare, and Mary would be getting flustered, getting the breakfast ready, all those men getting under her feet. She had better go in and help sort things out.

Master Standerby was feeling better this morning, at least he said he was. There was colour in his cheeks, and his eyes had a feverish brightness. Jennet did not like this, but he pooh-poohed the idea that he was ill. Over breakfast, which he ate heartily, he regaled them with anecdotes, repeatedly being capped by Harry, until there started a friendly rivalry between them. Harry was conscious, however, that this man would be his master, was in fact, even now, for the gentleman had, last evening, agreed to hire him on Jennet's recommendation, so he was careful not to go too far. But it was Christmas and things were allowed which would not normally be so.

After breakfast, Jennet decided that she and Mary could not possibly get their preparations started with four men, a lad and a little boy getting in their way. So, they were dispatched to their various rooms to change into their best clothes, if they had any, into clean clothes if they had not, and ordered into the parlour to amuse themselves as best they might. Master Standerby's clothes were now dry and clean, so he went up with Jack, Jamie and Harry and squeezed into Sam's room to change. Dickon, too, was washed and changed and directed to go in the parlour with the men, to his great delight. Roger was secretly amused, and pleased, to be included in this ordering. It made him feel as though he were one of them. He wished he felt better, though, he was beginning to get pains in his chest, and a slight headache. But he would not spoil their Christmas. He had half-heartedly declared this morning that he must go back to Whitegate Farm. He could not trespass on Mistress Towneley's generosity any longer. She rounded on him, exclaiming that it was Christmas and no one - *no one,* was going to leave her house on that day. He was to stay until all the festivity was over, and, she added archly, that could be until after New Year. He gave in, bowing gracefully to her wishes with a solemn face but inwardly congratulating himself. He also winced a little, hiding it carefully as he bowed.

So, he was usherered into the parlour with the rest, who had been given a jug of ale and cups, and extra seats, and stern instructions *not* to spoil her precious furniture. The carpet was rolled up, out of the way, and his camp-bed used to sit on.

Jennet and Mary set to, roasting and basting and making sauces, boiling vegetables and bringing out the goodies they had already prepared, for finishing touches. All this to shouts of laughter and merry voices issuing from the parlour. Jennet and Mary glanced often at each other as they worked and talked, indulgently smiling at the noise of their menfolk. Men were such children, they both agreed. But Jennet hoped the stories they were telling with such gusto were suitable for Dickon's ears, and perhaps to Jamie's, though, she surmised, there was not much that young man did not know.

When all was ready they called for volunteers to fetch in the old kitchen table from the dairy where it had been newly scrubbed the day before. They all volunteered, but Jennet picked out Harry and Jack as being the strongest. This was greeted with jeers from the unsuccessful ones. When it was brought in they were directed to place it at the end of the existing one, thus making one long table. The two men made offers of help in setting out the table, but were rejected and told to go back into the parlour until they were called, and to make sure they wiped their feet before doing so.

Mary and Jennet then brought out the white damask cloths which had been carefully packed away and brought out only on occasions such as this. Settling these carefully on the table, Jennet brought out some pewter candlesticks and set tall candles in them. She wished the candlesticks had been silver and that her dishes matched, but there was no use worrying about that now. And now for the food. There were capons and partridges, and roast pork with the crackling sizzling, beef pies and mince pies; the mince was meat finely chopped and mixed with spices and fruit, various sauces and dishes of peas and other vegetables, cabbage and turnips and the like. In between, Jennet set small dishes with sprigs of holly and mistletoe. Then she lit the candles and bade Mary announce that all was ready.

The men filed in and stood staring in admiration at the table. She briskly bade them be seated else the food would get cold. Sam, being the oldest, was asked to carve the first slices. He was considerably mellower than usual, having already partaken liberally of spiced ale. There were some bottles of wine and jugs of ale on the table and Roger, after asking Jennet's permission, rose to pour out the wine into each person's cup. He proposed a toast before they started to eat, to the two ladies who had worked so hard to make this sumptuous feast.

After that, there was not much conversation, except requests to pass this or that dish or platter of meat. Then Jennet and Mary went to get up to clear away the first course and to bring on the next, which was mainly fruit pies and syllabubs and the plum cakes, decorated with cream, and dishes of nuts and sweetmeats. But Roger commanded that they sit down and Jamie and he, and Master Dickon if he wished, would do the honours and the ladies should be waited on. They had worked hard enough.

And so they did, amidst much laughter and comments, not always complimentary, from the other men, at their adroitness or otherwise in handling the dishes.

Jennet then thought this was the happiest and merriest Christmas she had ever spent, and said so, smiling contentedly at them all.

After dinner was over they sat desultorily for a while, too replete to move. But Jack roused them, saying the animals must be seen to, Christmas or no. So putting on their outdoor footwear and pulling on woollen jerseys or jerkins, Sam and Harry and he trooped out.

Roger and Jamie and Dickon stayed to help clear away the tableware and remains of the meal and helped Jennet and Mary wash up. The old table was taken out, and the present one pushed against the wall and set again with dishes and platters of various meats and sweet dishes for them to partake of if they should desire during the evening. Roger went to see to his horse and found him munching placidly in the barn with old Betsey, now soon to be retired, but still cherished, and the other two horses, recently acquired, one for the ploughing and the other for drawing the wain.

The evening was as merry as the day had been. They played numerous games and once Jennet found herself seized from behind and turned to find a laughing Roger, holding a sprig of mistletoe over her. He bent swiftly and kissed her. She felt his lips burning on hers and was nearly overcome by a feeling of sweet languor that frightened and yet excited her.

Then the other men had to follow suit. Mary and she were assailed by all the men in turn, even Dickon was not to be outdone. But all she longed for was to feel Roger's arms about her again and his kiss on her lips. It was like nothing she had ever felt before. Richard's kisses had been sweet and tender, and she had loved him dearly. Unconsciously, her hand went to the locket at other throat. But, as her hand closed round it, she knew that he was aware of her feelings and approved of them. She felt as though a blessing had been bestowed on her. Her eyes went to seek Roger's. He was staring at her with a strange expression on his face, almost of pain. Then he straightened up and smiled gaily, saluting her with a wave of the hand and a slight bow.

The evening was over; wearily they sought their beds. The kitchen fire was banked and Jamie sent to make up the fire in the parlour. Roger sank on to his camp-bed, glad to be able to rest. He had not thought he could last out much longer. It was becoming difficult to breathe, and with each breath came a grinding pain in his chest. His head was pounding. . . .

Outside, the night was still, every sound muffled by the falling snow, now coming down thicker than ever.

CHAPTER NINETEEN

The next morning Roger could not rise from his bed. After the others had been up a while and were starting breakfast and he still had not appeared, they thought he was still feeling the effects of the previous night, and let him sleep for a while.

Then Jennet became anxious and sent Jamie in to waken him. The lad came back, grave and worried looking.

"He be ill, Mistress," he announced, "twas hard to wake him and his head is hot. He can hardly speak."

Jennet threw convention to the winds and hurried in, followed by Mary. She felt his forehead, it was burning. He struggled for breath and each breath brought him pain.

"He needs a physician," she said, and looked in despair at the still falling snow. The snow, which she had hoped would keep him there was now her enemy, effectively sealing them in from outside help.

"Well, we must do the best we can," she decided. "He must have my bed. It is more comfortable than this, and I will take this one and sleep in here. Dickon's bed must be brought in here, too." Again she gave orders to her willing band of helpers. First, the fireplace in her bed-chamber which had hardly ever been used, was filled with firewood and logs and lit. Dickon's small bed was brought out and installed in the parlour.

Dickon himself was highly intrigued by these manoeuvres and wanted to know why he was to sleep with Master Standerby. "You are not," replied his mother exasperatedly, "Master Standerby is ill and will be in my bed."

This was even more intriguing to the child. "But I thought only married ladies and gentlemen slept together. Are you going to marry Master Standerby, then? I should like that, I think."

Where he got his information about where married people slept she could only guess, and quickly assigned his friend, Jamie, who she thought was the source of this information, to explain the situation to him and keep him amused and out of the way. Jamie took him to his box-bed in the alcove, on which Dickon often played, drawing the curtain and pretending he was in an impregnable castle, besieged by foes. Here they ensconced themselves and were in a world of their own, while Jamie told him stories and fell in with his pretend game, where the scurrying figures outside the curtain became the enemy knights planning their destruction. When Master Standerby was carried through into his mother's chamber, he was, to them, a mortally wounded knight being carried away by his fellows from the scene of combat. His mother, hovering near, and directing Jack and Harry with their burden, was the knight's lady, tearfully bewailing her stricken lord's fall. Mary was, of course, the lady's maidservant and Jack, Harry and Sam, his faithful henchmen.

To Dickon, at least, it was an entrancing game, even Jamie, entering into the spirit of it was nearly convinced it was real. He had a wonderful imagination, had that boy.

If Jennet had known of their fancies, she might have also said how nearly true the analogy was. To her, Roger was indeed her lord, and how mortally stricken he was she could only conjecture.

His body was, like Dickon's and Jamie's beleaguered castle, being assailed by malignant unseen forces and she could only help in the smallest way his own bodily defence to withstand the siege. And she could pray - pray that God would not take him from her, too, as he had taken those others she had loved. Yes, she could admit it now. She loved him, and though it might have taken her longer to realise, would still have loved him even had he proved to be the cruel, vicious, unfeeling man she had once thought him to be.

When they had carried him through and laid him gently between the clean, warmed sheets of Jennet's bed, he was barely conscious. His half-closed eyes followed her about as she bustled about the room preparing a warm, healing posset. She tried to get him to drink it but he could only manage a little. He tried to speak, to tell her not to trouble herself over him, to thank her for her ministrations, but could only manage a whisper, which she had to bend her head close to his lips to hear. She bade him be silent and to save all his energy to combat the forces which were assailing him. He gave her the faintest of smiles, and very soon lapsed into unconsciousness.

For over a week, he lay thus, rallying occasionally, only to relapse again into fevered ramblings. He was icy cold and quilts and coverings were heaped upon him and the fire piled high, then he would throw them off, feverishly burning. His sheets had to be constantly changed as they grew wet through with his sweatings. Jennet grew desperate, trying to cope.

In his delirium, he often seemed to be in the midst of a battle (as he undoubtedly was, thought Jennet) and flailed his arms about as though wielding a sword. Sometimes, he called out names unknown to her and once for Elizabeth, who Jennet thought was his young, dead wife. Many times he spoke to John, who was his friend, as Aunt Meg had told her, and was killed in the war. She hoped that these, too, were fighting for him and prayed that they were. To Richard too, she said a prayer. She knew that this went against all the principles of her childhood's teaching, against her father's rigidly held views, but she did not care. She needed all the help she could summon to save this man. She realised that she did not even know his religion, had assumed he was Catholic, like Uncle Tom and Aunt Meg. But it did not matter any more. To most Presbyterians all Royalists were Papists, even though this was palpably untrue.

She kept her vigil then, bathing him with cool water to abate the fever and desperately trying to get him to drink or take nourishment. Mary came in sometimes, to relieve her and to beg her to take some food herself, but she could hardly tear herself away, returning in an hour or so to take up the fight again. The New Year came in, unnoticed. She grew pale and thin until Mary, worried sick herself remonstrated, saying she would fall ill herself, and then where would they all be?

The men were quiet, talking in hushed whispers and gazing mournfully at the snow, still falling fitfully. Even Dickon was subdued.

Then, on the eve of Jennet's birthday, it stopped, and the sun shone out. They all went out into the yard to try to clear it. They had had to keep a pathway clear to the shippon and the barn in order to minister to the animals and milk the cows. Mary exhorted them to be as quiet as they could, for the patient's sake. But as Jennet and she agreed, it would do them good to get out into the fresh air again and take some exercise.

He seemed a little better today, Jennet thankfully noticed, and going closer she saw that he was indeed asleep. His breathing was easier, too. She felt his forehead gingerly and yes - no - yes it *was* a little cooler! She started to send up a prayer of gratitude and then stopped halfway. She must not build her hopes up too soon. It could be just a few hours rallying and then he might sink again, deeper into the pit, as he had done before. But surely, it was true, he *was* better. She tried not to think about it and bent her head again to the sewing she was trying to apply her mind to. But her eyes hurt and she was so tired. She let the work fall to her lap and gazed towards the window. Through its dim panes she could just discern the sky. She saw the dark clouds massing. Oh, don't say it is going to snow again! she pleaded.

Suddenly, she was startled to see a great burst of snow smash against the window with a thud. They were snowballing! And Mary, on her orders, had told them to be as quiet as possible! With a muffled exclamation of outrage she got up to tell them what she thought of them when she heard a low chuckle. She turned her head incredulously, joyfully, to see him smiling at her.

"What, no snowballing for you today, Mistress?" he was asking weakly. With a great cry, she flung herself forward to clasp his wasted hand and kiss it, crying and laughing at once and murmuring her prayers of thankfulness. Mary rushed in a moment later, fearing the worst had happened. She saw her mistress's head bent over his hand and he, with the other, was stroking her hair. He looked at Mary's startled face and with an effort slowly winked.

Smiling, she closed the door quietly and was going out to tell the men the good news that Master Standerby was better, when they all came trooping in, trying hard to stifle their laughter as they shook their wet clothes. It was raining, and hard, too.

"Well if this keeps up, it will soon clear the snow away," said Jack, later that evening. "Happen then we can start the ploughing in time," he added with satisfaction. Mary edged nearer to him at the table. He smiled at her, thinking, what a good wife she would make for a farmer. They seemed to have grown closer to each other, since that day when the Mistress had made them tell of their experiences when the soldiers had raided their farm. Mistress had seemed happier, too, until Master Standerby was taken ill. There was no one like Mistress Jennet, he thought. She had always come first with him. Except perhaps. . . . He turned to look at the small fair head beside him, well perhaps now it would be this little lass here. She was a bonny 'un and no mistake, and she had worked like a little trooper this last week or so. He had thought perhaps she liked him, except when she had started making up to Harry Baines, but now she seemed to have forgotten *him.* Women were funny creatures, he reflected. He could never truly understand 'em. He had always thought he understood Mistress Jennet, but even she had her moods. Well, happen now Master Standerby looks as though he is going to get better, she will be as she used to be. Meanwhile, he and these others had better start thinking about their farm work. There could be some flooding if this snow melts quickly and the fields will be water-logged. The ditches will have to be cleared. Pity that Harry was going to work for Master Standerby, he could do with his help here for a while yet. Still, it looks as if he won't be wanted for a little time. Perhaps he could ask him to let Harry stay on here.

Jack's ruminations were interrupted by a radiant Mistress Jennet appearing at her chamber door.

"M-Master Standerby thinks he can take a little broth now, Mary," she said tremulously. "Can you fetch some please?"

Mary jumped up at once and fetching a dish, took some steaming broth from the pot hanging over the fire. "He must be feeling better, Mistress," she said gladly. "If he is hungry, 'tis a good sign." Jennet, smiling happily, took the dish and hurried back into the room.

Roger mended slowly over the next few weeks and by the middle of January he was well enough to forsake his bed during the day. He began to watch the weather and ask Jack if he thought the lanes would be fit enough for wagons to get through yet.

"You'll be thinking of your furniture and other stuff I reckon, Master," replied Jack, " 'tis a pity nothing could get through sooner with the snow first and then the rain miring up everything. But with this wind, and happen if we get a dry spell for the next few days, the roads will be passable."

Roger fretted and fumed, waiting anxiously to hear that there was a possibility of his goods arriving. He wanted desperately to get into his home and see his own furniture safely installed. There was the farm machinery, too. He'd ordered that when he had ordered the furniture. Jack had already started his ploughing; it was time to start on Whitegate Farm.

Jennet was hurt at his eagerness to leave them but there was not much she could do. Of course, she could keep him for a few days yet, he was not really fit enough to go out but his recovery was accelerating by the day. Since the day he had recovered consciousness, and she had so shamelessly thrown herself on him, there had been a constraint between them. She now felt that he must have been repelled by her conduct, or perhaps he just thought she was distraught by her days and nights of almost ceaselessly ministering to his needs and was over-tired and her protestations of joy and gratitude over his recovery were the expression of a kind-hearted and devoted nurse.

He was grateful, of course. Over and over he had thanked her, had thanked them all and declared he would never forget their unfailing kindness.

But now he wanted to be gone and had shown her clearly that he did not return her affection. She felt devastated, almost betrayed. But it was not his fault; how could he know? Yet had she imagined the feel of his hand stroking her hair, or his low whisper of her name? She could have been mistaken, overwhelmed with joy as she was. She was confused and hurt and retreated into a stony, resigned state.

Three days later, Thomas Trentham rode into the yard. Jennet ran to meet him, she had seen him from the kitchen window. Roger was behind her and went forward to take his friend's hand, after Jennet had embraced her uncle. She made him come inside at once, out of the biting wind and asked Jamie to see to his horse.

He would not go into the parlour but accepted a cup of wine and sat at the kitchen table, demanding to know how they had fared at Christmas and telling Roger that he had ridden up with the wagons of furniture for the house, which were even now waiting in the yard at Whitegate Farm for Roger's directions as to where to put each piece.

"When I found the house empty, I guessed you might be here, so rode over to acquaint you that your pieces had arrived. I presumed rightly, I see, that you were enjoying the hospitality of my dear niece, for you could not possibly live in that empty house."

Roger laughed and proceeded to tell him the whole story. Jennet listened in silence, her eyes downcast. When he had finished reiterating how he would have died, but for the devoted nursing of Mistress Towneley and her band of helpers, Uncle Tom turned to him with incredulity on his face.

"My dear Roger, how could you have put yourself into such a hazardous situation? When you told Meg and I that you wanted to spend Christmas in your own home, we assumed that you would have had adequate furniture and supplies to let you stay there in comfort. You know how we urged you to spend Christmas with us, but you, my impetuous and foolish fellow, were adamant. Meg will be aghast when she hears of this and will blame herself, for it was she who finally persuaded me that perhaps you should do as you thought best."

He did not add that Meg had decided that perhaps Roger and Jennet could be brought together by his being in the vicinity and no doubt calling on their niece. She had not given up by any means, hadn't Meg.

"And now, Roger," he continued, severely, "you have put Jennet and her household to untold trouble and worry over your illness and, I hope, you are as sincere as you seem in your protestations of gratitude, as well you should be."

Roger looked suitably chastened and assured her uncle that no one could ever know how much he was indebted to Mistress Towneley and that from henceforth he was her willing slave. She had saved his life and he could never discharge that debt. He held her and her friends, for that is what they had been to him, in the highest esteem and would do so for the rest of his life.

So that is what we are to him, thought Jennet bitterly. Friends, and that is well for them, no doubt, to be his friends. And I am included and it is not enough for me. But she spoke up calmly, deprecating his words, saying, "But we did nothing that any other Christian family would not do for a fellow human being in distress."

"You are too modest, my dear," Uncle Tom answered. "You must have worn yourself out, caring for this stupid fellow, for that is what he is, to cause such disruption by his own feckless behaviour." But his scathing words were offset by the look of affection he cast at his friend. "I can only thank God that it has turned out so well and must also tender my deepest thanks to you, Jennet."

"And now, with your permission, may we turn to the matter of your furniture, Roger? Those poor men are waiting for your directions and cannot be left there all day. Are you to come with me and see them?"

Jennet stepped in and said that Master Standerby was not yet fit enough to ride over in this cold wind and stand about directing workmen. "I will not answer for the consequences if he should get cold again, Uncle, and the house will be cold and damp, too."

"Then what are we to do, Niece," cried Uncle Tom, "the goods and furniture must be unloaded today."

Jennet made a quick decision. "Then if Master Standerby will permit me, I shall go with you and take Mary and Harry, and we will light the fires and get all cleaned and ready. This will take a few days but we will return here in time for supper each day. And now, Master Standerby, will you give Uncle Tom and me your requirements as to where the furniture should go?"

Roger had stood open mouthed, listening to her.

"Mistress Towneley, you will never cease to amaze me, you have already put me more in your debt than I can ever hope to repay and now this!. But I cannot allow you to do it. It is too much. No, I will go with Tom."

Her eyes blazed. "Sir, you will not! I have not saved your life, as you put it, for you to endanger it again. Come, Uncle Tom, we will go and if Master Standerby will not tell us where to put his things, then we will arrange them ourselves." With this parting shot, she snatched up her cloak from behind the parlour door and stormed out, calling for Mary and Harry to accompany her and to load the wain with wood and peat and brooms and all the other paraphernalia they would need.

Roger was thunderstruck and Tom, passing him, shrugged his shoulders and grinned, his expression conveying the thought - 'You'll have your hands full with that one my lad, but I envy you!'

Roger was thinking - By God, she is a wonder! There she goes, marshalling her troops again. What a fire-eating general she would have made, if she had been a man! But I am glad she is not. She is a queen and a beauty, too, with that fire flashing in her eyes. And had she but known it, I was going to consult her as to the arrangement of my house, for I want it to be as she would desire it.

CHAPTER TWENTY

They worked solidly for four days, returning home each evening, weary and grimy. On the first evening Mary and Jennet were not looking forward to starting all over again, preparing supper and doing their other chores, but were pleasantly surprised to find that Master Roger, too, had his organising abilities. They came in to find a blazing fire and the table set and pans and kettles on the hob filled with hot water for them to wash. The kitchen was clean and tidy and an appetising smell came from the oven. They sank down with relief on to the settle while Roger handed them each a cup of mulled ale to warm them and slake their thirst.

"Master Standerby, this is wonderful. But you should not have done it. You will over-tire yourself and undo all my good work." Jennet eyed him over the rim of the cup. He was standing there, looking a little tired but overwhelmingly pleased with himself.

"Mistress, I did nothing" - with an airy wave of the hand - "I have had much help from my two henchmen here" - the hand gestured towards Dickon and Jamie standing, grinning, beside him. "Master Dickon, it must be told, was averse to doing what he calls, 'woman's work', but my staunch ally, Sir James, turned it, with his usual imagination, into a game, and you will be surprised to learn that you are a victorious army returning from battle and we, the custodians of Castle Gregson, have been labouring to succour and feast you on your return, laden with the spoils of war."

He indicated the buckets and brooms they had brought in with them. They collapsed into helpless laughter.

"Well, Sir," said Jennet when she could speak, "I'll not deny it has been 'a battle' as you say, for it is amazing how much dirt can collect in a house when it has lain empty for months, and we must return to the fray for a few days yet for the battle is not yet over." She did not add that most of it was caused by the neglect it had suffered during the reign of Mistress Alice and her slovenly ill-disciplined servants. She went on to tell him that the workmen had returned to the house that day to finish the painting and repairs and other alterations he had ordered. "And that too is causing problems for we have to clean up after them. It may even delay our finishing our work, but they assured me that it would not take above a few days. Especially when I insisted on them continuing to work all through the day instead of breaking off every now and again for cups of ale and to take a bite of food, as they have, I assume, been used to doing. They grumbled, I assure you, but I soon put a stop to that. A man is entitled to his dinner, but his employer is also entitled to expect a fair days work and so I told them."

I can well believe it, he thought, smiling to himself. Aloud he said, "And now, my lady, if you and your attendants would care to use this plentiful hot water to cleanse and refresh yourselves, we can then repair to supper. My cooking will not be on a par with yours or Mistress Mary's, I daresay, but I trust it will suffice." He bowed low, continuing Jamie's game, and laughing, they went to their various rooms to take his advice.

It was quite a fair meal, they found, though as he was the first to admit, not up to their standard, but everyone was so hungry they devoured it with relish.

He was a strange man, Jennet was thinking, as she pushed her empty dish away. He could be charming and gay, almost courtier-like, or as she imagined a courtier to be, yet he could stoop to the level of a peasant and call them friends, and he could also fall in with Dickon's childish games, and to cap it all, take on a woman's work, which many men, even the commonest yeoman, would not deign to do. She was finding so many things out about him and liking them all. But he did not think of her, other than as a friend. Many times, though, she had looked up quickly and found him looking at her with a strange look in his eyes, but he had quickly turned away and made some laughing remark to the others, so she could never be quite sure of what he was thinking.

Well, he would be leaving soon, when his home was ready. She could make no more excuses for keeping him at her side. He would be eager to be off, she knew. Harry was going to stay there, and had been given instructions to recruit farm-workers from the neighbouring villages. There were many men returning from the army who would be glad of work, and Harry would also look out for a housekeeper and maidservants, although she thought Aunt Meg would like to do him this service. So she would do this one last thing for him, she who longed to serve him all her life. She would get his house clean and ready for him, perhaps for another woman who might one day be his wife. And then she would retire into the background; just a friendly neighbour whom she might visit occasionally to pass the time of day or discuss the state of their crops.

He left Gregson's Farm at the end of the week, vowing his eternal gratitude, and that their labour should not go unrewarded, promising also that the fuel and other items they had expended should be returned in full measure. Jennet protested at this, saying it was not necessary, for everything had been done, or given, with a good heart, and with no thought of return.

He said he knew this, but, nevertheless, they should not be the losers by it.

He bent over her hand, kissed it, and rode out, accompanied by Harry and Uncle Tom, who had ridden up from Preston, to see him into his new home. Aunt Meg, said Tom, would be calling on them both in the first fine day of spring.

They heard nothing more for two weeks. No word came from him, but Jack reported that wagons were arriving at Whitegate Farm on several occasions, and one day some arrived at their gate with a load of logs and some of that sea-coal which Aunt Meg had told her about. It came, said the carter, with Master Standerby's compliments, and that was all. Jennet had to admit that it was an improvement on their usual peat or wood fire, and seemed to last longer, and with more heat. She resolved to conserve it, for it was so expensive, and must be saved for special occasions. She wished, though, he had come himself, that would have pleased her far more.

On the eve of Dickon's birthday, she was busily engaged in making a special cake for her son, when Harry arrived, grinning from ear to ear.

He had been sent by his master, he said, to bid Mistress Jennet and her household to dinner the following day. He knew it was Dickon's natal day and begged her to allow him to provide the celebration, as some recompense for her care of him during his illness. He was sure she would allow her servants a holiday on this one occasion, and he would be very much affronted if they did not accept, and apologised for this short notice.

Harry recited this with some difficulty over the bigger words, and obviously had been carefully schooled, but he managed it at last and waited for her reply.

She was astounded, she had to admit, but pleased at the thought of seeing him again. Why had he not delivered the message himself? Still, like the beggar, she could not afford to be choosy. She *had* to see him again, this last two weeks had stretched interminably. How could she spend the rest of her life like this? And it would be a rare treat for Dickon, not to mention the others. To be invited out to dinner!

She knew they would quibble, and point to their rough clothes and rougher manners. But she would tell them that Master Standerby had not minded that when he was living in the same house as they were, so why should he mind in his own?

So, smiling at the eager Harry, she bade him tell his master they would be pleased to accept and would call on him on the morrow, at - what time? Yes, at one of the clock.

He was waiting in the doorway when they arrived in the yard at Whitegate Farm. He stepped out quickly and assisted Mary and Jennet to alight from the cart. Mary giggled delightedly, she was not used to being assisted from the wagon so courteously, and cast a meaningful glance at Jack, who blushed and shifted awkwardly on his feet. They were all a little constrained, even Jennet, for this was a situation entirely new to them. Roger could see this, and took great pains to put them at their ease.

Soon they were all laughing at his sallies, and Jennet took time to look at him closely. He was well but soberly dressed in a brown wool-cloth coat with gilt buttons and breeches of the same material. His shirt was white silk and she noticed the serviceable stockings over brown buckled shoes. Quite the country gentleman, he was, she thought, and so handsome she wanted to throw her arms around his neck and embrace him fiercely. He had evidently given much thought to his dress, she guessed rightly, not wishing to outshine his guests and yet do honour to the occasion.

Then they were in the house and even Jennet saw how much improved it was to when they had last left it. Everything was new and shining and the little maid who came forward, shyly curtsying, to take their outdoor things, was neatly and cleanly dressed. He showed them round, proud of his home and delighting in their cries of admiration.

Soon a solid, dour middle aged woman came in to declare that dinner was ready. She looked very disapproving at these upstarts whom her master had seen fit to invite as guests. She gave an audible sniff as she departed from the room. Roger looked displeased, but gallantly offered his arm to Jennet. The others followed. Jamie, imitating Roger, with a cheeky grin, offering his arm to Mary who took it, giggling, and glancing archly at Jack.

The room took their breath away, Jennet's more than anyone's, for, yes - it was the same room - or as nearly like it as made no matter - to the one she used to see in her girlish dreams, it seemed so long ago. A bright coal fire in the richly-carved fireplace, the tapestries on the walls, the polished sideboard, and the table! . . .

There were the silver candlesticks and silver dishes, all exuding a delicious aroma, on the snow-white lace-edged cloth. Roger told them where to sit, but Dickon he kept to the last.

"Now Master Dickon," he said, indicating the head of the table, "you are the guest of honour and this is to celebrate your birthday, so today you shall lord it over us all. Today you are King and we your loyal subjects, and your wish shall be our command."

Dickon, his eyes round, his face rosy with joy, climbed on to the ornate carved chair and sat, straight-backed, gazing imperiously around him at his 'subjects'. It was obvious he was already seeing himself in the role, and revelling in it. The housekeeper, if such she was, had been standing stiffly at the door, awaiting her master's orders, but he indicated that her services would no longer be needed and they would serve themselves. With evident relief, she departed. With her went some of the awkwardness they had felt in her presence.

Mary said self-consciously, "Ee, Master, I don't think I could eat a thing. It all be too grand for the likes of us. I be fair shaking, and shall drop something, I know it."

"Nonsense, Mary!" Roger laughed, "much finer things than these would not be too grand for you - or your mistress, - he raised a crystal cut glass to them both and drank deeply - "for you are of finer stuff than some of the greatest ladies in the land."

Jennet found his dark eyes staring straight into hers from where he sat opposite to her. What she saw there caused her face to flush and her heart to flutter wildly. She started to speak, and so did Harry and Jack, and soon they were all talking at once, affording her a chance to bring herself under control.

The meal went on, with much laughter and joking. Roger meticulously serving Dickon, as the guest of honour.

When they had eaten their fill, Roger excused himself and requested Dickon to follow him, with his mother, as there was something he desired to show them. The rest could stay and enjoy their wine at their leisure, which by their cheerful, relaxed faces, they were not averse to doing.

Puzzled, Jennet allowed him to lead Dickon and herself through to the hallway where he collected her cloak and Dickon's jerkin from the chest there. He took them outside, putting on his own cloak and leading the way to the stables.

When Dickon saw the pony, his face was a picture. Sleek and black, it stood nuzzling his shoulder. He stroked its velvet nose and beamed, eyes shining.

"Can I - May I ride it?" he breathed hesitantly.

"Yes, of course you may." Roger lifted him on to the pony's back. He sat, clutching the pony's mane, not daring to move. Roger watched him indulgently, then said quietly. "Do you like him, Dickon? His name is, - well, no matter what his name is, you may call him by whatever name you choose. He is yours, your birthday gift." The boy, unable to contain his delight, let out a whoop, and nearly fell off the pony, but for Roger's restraining arm. He lifted the child down. "When you have a proper saddle which I will have made for you, you will learn to keep your seat. Now talk to him and let him get used to you, while I have a word with your mother."

Jennet had let out a gasp of surprise at his statement and was about to say he should not give Dickon such an expensive present, that he was spoiling the lad and . . .

But her thought and her speech were stopped by Roger's hand drawing her away to the other end of the stable. She allowed him to lead her, without further protest. But she was shaken to the roots of her being, when his arm closed round her and she heard a low vibrant voice telling her he loved her, had loved her since the day he had first seen her. She returned his kiss, feeling herself drowning in a sea of emotion. Then, when a degree of sanity returned - it seemed like a thousand years had passed and yet a split second of time - she pushed him away and demanded, "Why then, if you have loved me for so long, have you only now decided to tell me? If you knew how I have suffered, thinking you had no such thought for me. Sir, you are an unfeeling beast as I first thought you."

He stopped her with another kiss.

"So, my little, precious Jennet, you do love me. I have hardly dared to hope, and yet, sometimes it seemed you regarded me kindly. When I was ill I heard your voice whispering endearments, then when I was better, you were distant again and I thought it was a dream, part of my delirium brought on by my own longing."

"Rog - Roger," she hesitated over his name, but she whispered it so many times in her mind, so why not say it now? "Roger, you have not yet answered my question."

"Your question, my love?" He looked at her blankly, then remembering said, his lips against her cheek. "Because, my sweet Jennet, I dared not declare my love, when I was still a homeless man. I vowed I would not speak until I could bring you to my own home, to our home, and it seemed hopeless, until by a stroke of good fortune, my small inheritance, which I had wisely invested, showed some profit, and is still bringing me a small, but adequate return. Hence all this," he waved an arm vaguely, "but there was something you said, was there not?" He thrust her out at arms length, studying her quizzically. "You said - that at first you thought me an unfeeling beast. Why was that?"

Jennet did not want to tell him just then. She could not spoil this moment. Oh, why had she blurted it out? Mayhap, later she would tell him.

"Oh, it was nothing, just a slip of the tongue. I-I didn't - " she faltered, unable to go on.

He was going to insist that she tell him. He knew there was something there, by her voice.

And as he glanced down, there was Dickon gazing at them interestedly, his hands on his hips, and he had obviously been there for some time.

"Are you going to get married, then?" he enquired, with the engaging frankness of the young. "I saw you kissing Mam and Mary told me that when a man kisses a lady they should get married. Are you then, and will you then be my father?"

Roger bent and picked him up.

"Would you like that, Dickon? Would you like me for a father?"

The boy squirmed in his arms. "Yes sir, I - I think so, I like you very well. But sir - if you do not mind, I think I like the pony better. I shall call him Lionheart, you know, after the King Mammy told me of."

And so she never told him of the hate she had once felt for the Roger Standerby of 1643, and he was wise enough not to press her for the story. Mayhap later on, when they were a sedate married couple, secure in their love and in their marriage. Meanwhile, the Roger Standerby of 1648, thought of what the repercussions might be of King Charles' escape to the Isle of Man and his negotiations with the Scots to help him regain his former power. Would there be another Civil War? He prayed not, for he did not want to leave his bride, his lovely Mistress Jennet. If war came again he would have to fight for his King, and heaven knew what could happen to them both.

But that is another story.

****

Master Roger

A sequel to 'Mistress Jennet' is
planned, written by
Marjorie Hull, entitled 'Master Roger'.
Set in the 17th century,
it continues the story of Jennet
and the trials and tribulations in
those troubled times.

Publication is planned for 1998.